GOOD GIRL
GONE BAD

A DIRTY DEBTS NOVEL

D1523215

GOOD GIRL GONE BAD

A DIRTY DEBTS NOVEL

CARMEN

USA TODAY BESTSELLING AUTHOR

FALCONE

Entangled Publishing, LLC
644 Shrewsbury Commons Ave
STE 181
Shrewsbury, PA 17361
rights@entangledpublishing.com

Scorched is an imprint of Entangled Publishing, LLC.

Edited by Alethea Spiridon
Cover design by LJ Anderson/Mayhem Cover Creations
Cover art from Faferek/Getty Images

Manufactured in the United States of America

First Edition April 2018

entangled
scorched

To my besties Kristina Redmon and Marci Protsman. I love our girl dates!

Chapter One

Go screw yourself.

Marco Giordano read the text he'd received from Elizabeth. Of course, she'd already told him that an hour earlier when he'd proposed she sign a contract to become his temporary fiancée.

Sighing, he slid his Lamborghini into the parking lot of a strip mall.

What else could he do? In two weeks, his grandmother would turn ninety years old. He hadn't planned on attending her birthday—hadn't in several years—but a phone call from his cousin changed his resolve. Nonna wasn't just celebrating a milestone. Due to illness, she'd most likely be celebrating her last year of life. Maybe even her last month.

He parked his car and sat for a moment. His gut clenched like someone had punched him. What a joke. Due to his size and martial art skills, a man would be an idiot to raise his voice to him, let alone hit him. Marco ran his fingers through his hair. He would take any beating, anything to buy his precious Nonna more time from her congestive heart failure.

I should have visited more often. I should have been there for her.

He hadn't been, and she could never find out the reason why he'd avoided her for years—that alone could kill her.

Shaking his head, he slid out of the car and shut the door behind him. His brother Nico had told him about this place, a small, rundown strip mall. It was strategically located in an area they planned on revitalizing into a cool shopping and restaurant oasis. A hip district. Their representative had been able to convince the owners to sell their retail spaces to them… Well, all but one.

Now he had to talk to Lily Jenkins, the owner of a hair salon. She'd also been stirring up controversy, telling the other owners not to sell and trying to stall negotiations.

Why did this matter?

He could simply send a lawyer to tell her that her chances of winning this battle were nonexistent. He'd looked into her situation. At one point, her family had owned the entire mall, but over the past several years they'd sold each office space to an investing company or direct buyer. This was the last piece of property she possessed. With the amount of debt she owed, most likely she couldn't even afford an attorney. Yet, a part of him preferred to speak to her in person because he didn't want bad PR. As much as he knew he was right, only one bad tweet in the world of social media could make people second-guess their opinion about an entire company. He didn't want any dark clouds hanging over him before Nonna's birthday. That meant avoiding negative headlines.

He'd been absent. Now, he'd make it up to his grandmother even if was that last thing he did for her—he'd show up with a good-looking lady he'd claim as a fiancée, too. Show his grandmother he'd marry someday. His nonna had always bugged him about settling down, and even if it were a false pretense, he'd fake it for her. Hell, he'd hire a struggling, unknown actress to play the part.

Marco strode by the boutiques and massage parlors until he reached the last shop in the strip. A sheer leopard-print curtain adorned the window. The space was small compared to others in the area—certainly minuscule compared to the place on Madison Avenue where he'd gotten his last haircut.

Still, there was a kitschy charm about the salon. He knocked on the glass door, but a petite woman with a colorful apron simply gestured for him to come inside. The woman. His heart skipped a beat.

She had to be Lily Jenkins. Due the size of the place, he doubted she could afford employees.

"Welcome," she said. "I'll be with you in a minute."

Her green eyes twinkled, and he wondered if he'd ever seen a pair with such beauty. Specks of gold flickered around the irises, where a ring of avocado green encircled a brighter emerald color.

For the first time in his life, words failed him. He parted his lips to speak, but a huge lump in his throat prevented him from saying anything. He swallowed hard and cleared his throat. A sound finally traveled from the depths of his lungs, his voice coarse. "Hi."

"Please sit down," she said, gesturing at the chair in front of the large mirror. "I've been waiting for you."

She had? Maybe Nico had mentioned his issues with her standoff, though he'd texted his brother and told him he'd take care of her personally. Patience had never been his brother's forte, though, so maybe he had called Lily to warn her Marco would drop by.

"I have to say, I didn't expect such a tall guy. What are you? Six two?" she asked, and before he responded, a black smock swooshed over him.

"Six four," he said, straightening his shoulders.

"Whoa. That's amazing."

When she closed the smock's snaps, her fingers brushed the hairs on the back of his neck. The simple, accidental touch ignited a fiery response. His internal temperature raised to scary levels, and his groin stirred. God. She even smelled amazing—a mix of floral and spicy notes.

"So, what are we going to do today?" She played with his hair. "I like your current cut... How about we wash it, then figure it out? Maybe just a trim?"

"Sounds good," he said, his brain fogged by the sultry way her fingers worked his head. Maybe she wanted to give him a haircut first to show him how talented she was and how she needed to keep her business.

With a gesture, she told him to head to the only washing station. For the second time since their brief meeting, he followed her lead, somewhat entranced by her.

He tried to adjust to the chair in front of the sink.

"Sorry. These were not made for a big man like you, right?" she said, then chuckled nervously.

Did she feel it, too? This animalistic attraction expanding between them? He placed his head back, and soon warm water deluged his hair. In an attempt to regain his typical control, he closed his eyes, willing himself to relax. She applied shampoo and lathered his hair. Then...

She began slow, languid strokes on his scalp. His cock strained against his pants, and blood boiled in his temples. She continued the motion, massaging his head, her rubs firm and deep. His scalp sizzled with awareness, the sensation shooting down his body and searing every cell in its path. When heat coiled low in the pit of his stomach, his hard-on reached a painful level.

He suppressed a groan. *Dio.* He should stop this game, surge to his feet, and tell her who he was and what he'd do to her—but he knew when he told her, she'd hate him. Selfishly, he needed her hands on him for a bit longer. Never had a woman evoked such erotic reactions from him so quickly, with his clothes still on and without any intimate touch.

Though, her hands washing his hair then reapplying a creamy conditioner were living proof intimacy didn't need nakedness. He opened his eyes for a moment, stealing a glance at her. He'd expected her to engage in small talk, but he found her alluring eyes riveted on his. Her lips parted as if she yearned for a lover's kiss.

His kiss.

She removed the conditioner, her actions robotic and calculated as if she were in some kind of a trance. Damn it.

Pre-cum coated the tip of his cock, and he had never been so grateful for a stylist's smock. Not that she wouldn't be able to see his hard-on if she glanced down. She grabbed a towel from a shelf behind her and started to dry his hair. Again, her hands on him did a number to his usually remarkable self-control.

"Now I need you back at my station," she said.

He didn't miss the note of apprehension in her voice. "My pleasure," he said, following her lead. At first, the salon hadn't seemed so minuscule, and now the walls seemed to close in on him as he sat down.

She stood behind him, smoothing her apron more than once. "What do you want?" she asked.

Smiling inwardly, he doubted she was talking about the cut. "I want you."

• • •

Lily stood motionless, her feet pinned to the spot like the roots of a decades-old tree. She didn't dare yank her gaze from the mirror where the reflection of that marvelous specimen of a man stared at her, challenging her with every passing nanosecond.

What the hell was going on? She'd been on a dry spell for months, not interested in dating. Not that her busy schedule left much time for anything else but work—after she'd returned to the salon, she'd tried finding new clients. She'd gone to trade shows, taking workshops. All had gone well until a big salon franchise had opened across the street, and just like that, her hard work had turned into dust.

And now her body was a hot mess. Strands of heat charged within her, bolting down until it reached the wet place between her legs. Yep. Her clit throbbed in anticipation, as it had from the first moment she laid her eyes on this man. The man...who certainly wasn't the guy her friend Tony referred to her as a potential client. Tony had told her he'd given her business card to a guy he met at a club. A guy whose name he didn't remember. She hadn't asked this hottie's name, afraid she'd make it awkward for Tony if she admitted he hadn't remembered the name. What if the two had hooked up? Instead, she'd hoped he would pay with a credit card so she'd discover his name in a more discreet way, without throwing her friend under the bus.

"You're not gay, are you?" she asked for the sake of asking. She had her share of gay friends and loved every one of them. She could bet there was nothing but dangerous maleness about the object of her desire.

He'd dwarfed her when he'd stood, but now, even sitting, he had the commanding vibe of royalty, of someone who could snap his fingers and fulfill his wishes. Besides needing a trim, his cut was perfect, the chestnut hair falling down on his ear, textured and sexy. She had indulged herself when she washed his hair, and wondered how nice it would be to do the same thing with his body, smoothing lather over his ridiculously broad shoulders and muscly chest just as she'd done with his thick, gorgeous hair.

He gave a hearty laugh. "No."

Shit. If he'd been gay, her stomach wouldn't be in knots. He wasn't the one Tony had said would stop by for a cut. Which meant today she was clientless, another day without making any money. Concern squeezed her heart. The last couple of weeks, her one worry had been how to keep her head above water.

The compliments she'd given him about his height and hot maleness stabbed at her. What if he judged her to be some hairdresser who flirted with every guy just to get a good tip? No. "Oh. I'm sorry… Listen, I was joking around. I thought you were someone who was supposed to come over for a cut. And he's gay."

"Are you disappointed I'm not gay, *cara*?" he said in that deep, exciting, dreamy accent.

She sucked in her breath, bottling her reply and buying some time. Then she shifted her weight from one foot to another, unsure, feeling ten years younger. "No," she confessed, her throat dry.

A powerful energy passed between them as they stared at each other. Fire brewed at the pit of her belly. God. She was going to die soon if he didn't kiss her. What was happening? She usually had a five-date rule before she'd even go to second base, and now she stood in front of this stranger, her nipples tightening and her pussy wet.

He swiveled on the chair until he faced her, then pulled her to his lap, and she didn't resist. She didn't have it in her to fight this incredible attraction that sent electrifying ripples through her. He positioned her so she straddled him, and when she adjusted, a large rod poked against her. For once, she was thankful for her lack of clients and her empty shop. Heat seeped through the flimsy material of her underwear, and she gasped. When he'd been on the washing station, she made an effort not to look directly at his erection.

Now she couldn't ignore it.

"Good. I want you nothing but satisfied," he said, then lifted a finger to her face. The moment his thumb stroked her cheek, a part of her melted like ice cream on the pavement on a torrid summer day.

Blood pounded in her veins. She leaned into his caress, reveling in the warmth of his flesh and the goose bumps it provoked in her own. *I deserve this.* She'd spent her free time during the past three years taking care of her sick father. She'd seen their assets evaporate to pay for his treatment, then for her mother's surgery and retirement home costs.

His finger slid down the corner of her mouth, and she smiled. He traced her lips with his fingertip, his gaze transfixed on hers. She didn't manage to escape the undeniable appeal of his rich chocolate eyes.

His hand slid down, touching her neck, teasing the side of her breast, then he settled at the small of her back. A gentle but firm pressure pulled her closer to him, and soon he shifted on the chair and brought them to a sinful mold.

Her heart throbbed at the base of her throat, and she shut off everything around them. He captured her lips with his, and her world as she knew it collapsed beneath her. She opened her mouth to allow him full access, and he took every single bit of it. His tongue stroked hers with passion and urgency, the kiss growing hungrier than a ten-day fasting diet.

He placed his hand on the back of her neck, his fingers kneading her skin. Any kinks she might have had from moving stuff around her apartment dissolved under the power of his hand. Between kisses, a moan flew from her lips. Her hot stranger and possible potential client took it as encouragement, crushing his mouth on hers again, intensifying the kiss as if breathing became a luxury neither of them could afford.

She squirmed in his lap, and even though she was on top, he had complete control of the situation. It felt damn good not to worry about a thing. Constant insecurities of career, income, and worse, the bullying real estate company that wanted to buy her space, disappeared. She needed this, needed him.

"*Bellissima.*"

She opened her mouth to reply, but again he disarmed her with the intensity of his eyes. Nothing that she'd say, no snarky remark could ever be a match to his enticing accent. He looked at her like she was a big deal. Hell, she felt like one.

He kissed her again, their tongues caressing each other with the intimacy of old lovers reunited. Nonsense. If she had met a man as arresting as this one before, she'd damn well remember. In one swift movement, he stood up and took her with him. She wrapped her legs around him, giggling, as he carried her to her tiny bathroom/supply room. If she'd cursed the area for the lack of space before, now she welcomed it.

He positioned her on the top of the sink without slowing down the kiss. If anything, it grew stronger, greedier, more urgent. When he reached to her back to undo her apron, she realized his fingers trembled. Desire renewed at her core, and she reached for his hands, giving them a small squeeze. God. Was this really happening? After no sex for almost three years, she was fucking a complete stranger in her place of work?

He lowered the apron until it bunched at her waist, then cupped her breasts over the buttoned white shirt she'd chosen. She arched her back, bucking into him so he'd end her agony.

"*Dio mio…* You're so fucking sexy. What am I going to do with you?"

"Nothing too virtuous I hope."

He chuckled.

"I'm just saying it'd be a hell of a disappointment if you brought me all the way here to hand me your business card or tell me you're married." She straightened her shoulders. "You're not, are you? Married?"

He shook his head, lifting up her skirt. God. Goose bumps rose wherever he playfully touched her. Blood boiled at a pulse behind her knee she'd never even noticed she had. All of her roared in a silent plea for this man, this man who thankfully wasn't married, to take her.

He continued to make his way up her thigh until his finger slid beneath her underwear. She wished she wore something sexier than the faded blue hipster pair, but he didn't seem to mind. She moaned when he found her engorged clit, her nub vibrating at his touch.

He explored her pussy, his fingers rubbing her folds, and she rode his hand, undulating her hips at every advance. No doubt he had skills, his deft thumb flicking her in a mad rhythm, on par with his three fingers sliding in and out of her, claiming her, each time deeper, faster.

Moans fled her lips, and soon ripples of pleasure washed through her, making her shake into his arms. Sweat slicked and freshly fingered, she could barely breathe. "God. This... is...was..."

"I know, baby," he said, then rested his forehead against hers. But she needed more. She wanted him completely inside her, and quick. What should have ended her thirst for him only enhanced it.

She touched his belt, fumbling to open it. "Do you have a condom?" she asked, giving herself a mental high-five for asking such a critical question when her mind was nothing more than a glorious fog.

"Yes," he hissed out then fished his wallet from his pocket.

She unbuckled his belt, and while he grabbed the foil packet and tore it open, she slipped her hand into his boxer briefs. Wow. A hot, enormous cock vibrated in her palm, and she licked her lips. How on earth would she fit all that… meaty goodness into her sex? She clutched it, reveling in the velvety skin and thick girth.

He withdrew himself from her to roll on the condom. Her sigh filled the air, those two seconds stretching into eternity. He flashed her a devilish grin, as if he knew exactly what she was thinking.

She willed that thought away. Screwing this sexilicious man was about having fun, enjoying it, not making demands.

He dipped his head down, and she linked her arms around him. "You're killing me, but it's going to be a sweet death."

"The French call it a small death," she said, wrapping her legs around his torso.

He kissed her nose, sending all kinds of toe-curling thrills through her. "I'll make sure it's a big one for both of us." Maybe he used the sweet caress as distraction as he positioned his rod at her entrance and slowly rubbed the fat head on her folds.

"Hope you're not overselling yourself."

He traced his tongue over her neck, causing a bolt of adrenaline to almost combust in her veins. "Never, *cara mia*, never."

She shivered and lifted her eyes to him. She found him grinning, watching her intently. Silently, he asked her if she was ready for more. As a response, she shifted a bit to accommodate his cock. He curled his lips and drove his dick inside her.

At every inch, she made herself a mental note to relax and enjoy. Her walls clung to his flesh, and when he finished entering her, she gasped. An ache stabbed at her. God, he was big. Sweat slicked her forehead and neck. For a few seconds, they remained joined, still, and her pussy produced another coat of her pearly essence as if her body knew she needed to have him.

"You're big," she said, doubting he'd never heard it before. Now he was with her, inside her, and she refused to think of him pleasuring any other woman, though, she was sure he had...

"And you're tight, but we'll figure it out," he said, and captured her lips in another long kiss. He nibbled her upper lip and lifted his hand to cup her breast. Soon, her shoulders dropped a notch, and she felt him moving inside her.

She wrapped her legs around him more tightly for support. She loved the sensation of being completely filled by him. With his other hand, he began to touch her hot bundle of nerves. She wished he weren't so good at it. He worked her clit, his thumb flicking, pinching it without relent. He amped up the rhythm of his thrusts, each time withdrawing his dick faster and fucking her deeper, all the way to the hilt.

He stopped caressing her breast and lifted her left leg, stretching it so her ankle rested on his shoulder. "Fucking hot," he groaned, and this time when he continued the torturous in-and-out dance, he rammed into a profound place inside her.

She let out a raw moan, her heart about to burst in her ears. Thumps of each beat became louder. She knew she was stretching to the max to accommodate him, their contact airtight. "So. Deep," she said, barely choking out the words.

"I know, *tesoro*." His voice was gruff, haunted, and erotic. She had no idea what his occupation was, but he could definitely moonlight as a sex phone person and make buckets of money from his accent alone. "I'm feeling it, too... I love being inside you."

He nibbled her lip again, his teeth grazing her flesh. She slipped her fingers into his shirt, feeling his amazing shoulders, the taut muscles tensing under her touch. She bet he looked like an Adonis 2.0 when naked, but right now they were both too turned on to even take off their clothes. She scratched his skin, squeezing him closer. He let out a couple of groans and retaliated, fucking her faster, intensifying that pull and push about to drive her insane.

Her breath came out in bursts, and soon pleasure exploded in her pussy, sending charges of heat through her. She clutched him, coming undone in glorious, long-lasting spasms like nothing she'd ever experienced.

"That's right," he said, pumping harder into her, his heavy, full balls slapping her sticky thighs as he claimed her.

She was barely getting over the orgasm when he resumed his sweet torture of her clit, and suddenly, the climax reignited and her body sizzled again. Confused, she embraced him for support, unsure if she was still peaking from last time or if this was a bonus.

"Next time I fuck you, I want to come all over you. On your big tits, deep in your sweet pussy, on your ass, in your mouth. I want to coat you with my cum so there's no doubt where you belong."

His dirty words ripped her apart, like she approached a cliff, and they pushed her over the edge. She closed her eyes and fell hard, her body convulsing. She opened her mouth to call out his name, but only managed to choke out a whimper. He growled before releasing himself into her, shivering.

Then he planted a kiss on her forehead, and she blinked. No, this hadn't been some crazy erotic dream. She had just been freshly fucked by a man who she'd never met before. A man whose name she didn't know. A walk-in client.

"I have to ask. What brought you to my salon?"

Chapter Two

Marco ran his fingers down his face. The post-climatic haze cleared out of his head as he withdrew from Lily then removed the condom and threw it in the tall, lined trash can. She pulled down her apron and smoothed her hands over it, and he almost wished he could take her again.

In less than two minutes she'd hate him. When he told her he was here to buy her salon, she'd be furious. And even then… Even with that possibility, his body still throbbed and tingled. His mind might catch up with reality, but the most honest part of his hadn't. Screwing her hadn't sated his hunger; it only worked as an appetizer for the exquisite banquet he planned to feast on. That he *would* feast on.

"What?" she asked, sensing his hesitation. She walked to the door and returned to the shop's interior. "Why did you come here? You don't need a haircut, do you?" she said, tossing him a glance over her shoulder.

He followed her out of the bathroom. After what they'd shared, she deserved nothing but the truth. "No." He stalked toward her as she turned around and faced him. "I'll start with my name. I'm Marco Giordano."

She tilted her head to the side. "I'm Lily Jenkins. Should I know who you are?"

"Frank Stewart has been in touch with you," he said, grateful his trusted employee had kept their identity undercover for the time being. He and Nico didn't like revealing themselves until it was strictly necessary. People could use his family's wealth as leverage for asking for more money, just because they had it. Using a third party made more sense.

In slow motion, Lily stepped back, the contours of her face hardening. The soft, warm, willing woman he'd just screwed disappeared. Disappointment flickered in her eyes. Marco's spine locked into place, tension brewing in his gut. "You want me out of the shop?" she asked.

"I know it's a lot to take in, but yeah… Everyone else in the strip mall has agreed to sell their suite."

She folded her arms over her chest. "Well, I haven't."

"I understand, but you're behind on paying your bills. Even if we didn't insist on doing this, you'd have maybe, what? One, two months? Three, tops, until you file for bankruptcy."

She flattened her lips with a slow shake of her head. "I can't believe this. You walk in here, hit me with your good looks and devil dick, and expect me to hand you the key to my suite? A place that was passed on to me from my parents?"

"Lily, when I came in here, I didn't have an evil plan to sleep with you," he said, for the sake of being proper, even though they technicality hadn't slept. "I wanted to talk to you about your situation and help you see you're better off selling your suite to us. We're offering you well over the market value, and I'm willing to increase the offer."

"No. I don't need your charity. You used me," she said, then erased the distance between them and slapped her palm on his cheek.

Merda. His skin stung a little, but the fact she slapped him awakened a reaction other than pain. His body roared, recognizing her touch even if in a much different way than minutes earlier. Renewed desire charged through him. Lily was passionate, vibrant, downright sexy—and she belonged in his bed.

"I didn't come in here with the intention of seducing you. I apologize for not making it clear who I was, but who cares? Once we laid eyes on each other, nothing else mattered," he said, holding her gaze. "If I have a devil dick, you have a heavenly pussy."

An adorable wave of red spread across her cheeks and neck, a telling fact that she at least agreed with him on their strong pull. "Well, it happened. We'll have to get over it and move forward."

"I don't want to get over it. I want to relive it. To do it again and again."

She shrugged. "Tough luck."

Maybe Elizabeth was right. His life would be easier if he didn't need a contract for everything. The teenage boy in him, the one who took his father to a rehab clinic, disagreed. Contracts, for everything, made his life less complicated. He knew what to expect and what to give—without that structure, he'd be vulnerable to a give-and-take dynamic, and he'd lose. "I have a proposition for you. You have a debt that's going to suck you dry. Let me take care of it. I'll pay all your debts and find you another place nearby."

She stood, hands perched at her waist. "It won't be my mother's. I used to come to this same place as a little girl. I once broke my arm running on that sidewalk," she said, pointing to the window. "I won't ever have the connection I have to this place somewhere else."

He curled his fingers into a ball then uncurled them quickly. The sad look on her face made him want to rush to comfort her, but he had to be strong. Sentimentalism had no place in the business world. Another lesson his father had taught him early in life. "No, but it'll be a more modern setup, in a better neighborhood, in a place that'll give you more chances to succeed."

She unfolded her arms and let them fall to her sides. "Why can't I succeed right here?"

He perched his hands at his waist. A pang of frustration stabbed at him, but he breathed in and out quickly and continued. "Because I need the space to make a garage for the restaurants, shops, and the entertainment area we're creating. This exact location is perfect. Think about all the jobs we'll offer to those who need to work."

"All the jobs? Like you care about the common man? You must be joking. Besides, even if I sell it to you, I won't be able to afford a place like one of those you mentioned."

"Yes, you will. I'll…give you money," he said, the words escaping his mouth without his permission. Shit. Moments with her and he was already making bad business decisions.

She threw him a skeptical look. "Why would you do that?"

Wheels began to turn rapidly in his brain. If he helped her financially, what could he possibly ask for? He cleared his throat. "Because I want something in return."

"Ah. Of course. There's no such thing as a free lunch. What can I possibly offer you?" she asked, unruffled.

What indeed? His lip curled into a smile. She'd be shocked in a second or two, but he needed to finish his proposal. Contracts dictated his life, so why not make a dirty one? "I want your body in my bed. One month. Then I'll move you to a place where clients will appreciate your talent." *And I'll never bother you again.* Certainly, four weeks would be enough to water down the fire between them.

She lifted an eyebrow. "I'm not a hooker."

"No, you're not. You're a brilliant woman, who's also very proud. You're a woman who excites me in a way I haven't been in a long time. I don't mean to offend you. Let's say we're two regular people who met through mutual friends or at a bar. We date for one month, figure out we're not a match outside the bedroom. It could happen. What would we get in the end? False hopes and heartbreak at best. What I'm doing is ensuring you'll get the backup you deserve in this shitty situation, while I get what I need," he said, remembering the abandonment with which she'd come in his arms. His pulse raced with the image alone. He couldn't wait to have her come again, several times. He couldn't wait to savor her over and over.

"You talk like this is a business deal."

He reached into his inside pocket and grabbed a business card. The dynamics of the boardroom had taught him to keep his poker face. If she knew how much he wanted her to say yes, she'd have the upper hand. "It is. I'll draw up a contract. Two, in fact. One is a confidentiality agreement, and the other one states you'll be mine sexually—only mine—and I'll give you what you want at the end of the month."

"What you're offering isn't what I want."

He grabbed a pen and added his personal cell phone number to the back of the card. When he stepped forward to give it to her, she jerked away, as if the minimal contact with him would start a chain of events she'd rather crush. "It's the best offer you can get. I'll pay all your debts, pay well above market value for your space, and set you up in a coveted location."

She shot him a mocking smile. "An Italian knight in white and shining armor saving me from harm all because of my heavenly pussy. The stuff Shakespearean poems are made of."

He suppressed a chuckle, intent on showing how serious

he was about his proposal, and put his business card on the shelf. "I'm giving you twenty-four hours to consider my offer. After that, it's off the table."

· · ·

"Hi, Mama." Lily walked into the nursing home's shared living area. Several folks talked either to each other, or to the TV displaying a daytime talk show. She had wanted to bring her mother flowers, but for the past few weeks she'd been saving however she could.

"Hi, sweetie," her mother said, and when she stood from the recliner chair, she did so more slowly than usual, her hand resting at her hip.

"Are you okay?" Lily asked. Her mother sure looked younger than her seventy-one years, as Estelle Jenkins had always taken good care of herself. After her husband's death a year and a half ago, she'd decided to go to a retirement community where she'd still be pretty independent but would have help if needed, especially after a hip replacement surgery and other age-related health concerns.

Estelle waved her off. "I'm fine, honey. I attended a beginner's ballroom dancing class yesterday and am paying the price now."

"Mom... Be careful."

Estelle's blue eyes sparkled. "I've been careful my whole life, dear. Wife of a pastor. Can't a girl have some fun?" She winked with her trademark wit, and Lily's heart squeezed in her chest.

She gave her mom a hug that lasted longer than intended, finding comfort in the warmth of her embrace. When she disengaged, Estelle looked at her with concern. "What is it, munchkin?"

Well, munchkin is broke and about to sell her soul

to the devil. Lily ran her fingers into her hair, messing up her ponytail. If Marco had meant it, she had just over two hours to make the decision that could change her life and corrupt every value her father had instilled in her. Maybe she deserved it—if she hadn't screwed Marco, she wouldn't know what it was like. The way he touched her and made her feel would be enough reason for *her* to pay *him* for a screw—if she could afford it.

"Is it a man? Did my Lily finally meet someone special?" Her mother smiled, and they walked through the Japanese-themed gardens.

"I'm not sure special is the word. I'm not ready to talk about him or anything," she said, glancing down at the pebbled path.

Estelle chuckled. "I'll take that as a yes. You know, when I met your father, I wasn't a practicing Christian. I was scared, at first, because he felt so strongly about what he stood for. I didn't know if I could live up to that."

"How did you know?"

"I gave it a shot," Estelle said. "I don't regret it. Your father gave me everything I needed. By the way, how's the salon?"

"Oh. It's doing well." Lily used the same response she'd given her mom for months. Her heart burned with regret every time she'd said it, but she refused to say anything else until she clawed her way out of the mess she was in. She'd seen how selling her family's assets had devastated Estelle, and she'd promised her mom—and herself—after Dad's funeral, she'd do whatever she could to always keep the salon. That part of their past wouldn't, couldn't, be destroyed.

"Maybe one of these days you can take me back for a day trip," Estelle said. Once a month in the past year, Lily had summoned Estelle's clients from back in the day and brought her mom for a fun "girl's day" at the salon she'd called home for decades.

"Yes, we'll arrange something." Fear churned in her stomach. In less than two years, her mother had lost her husband, battled breast cancer, then endured a hip replacement surgery. She'd left their house and moved into the retirement home. She'd lost so much, yet kept positive, in high spirits—no doubt always looking forward to those days when she visited her old stomping grounds and remembered the occupation she dearly loved. What if she had to give that up, too?

"Good. I was telling Jeff, the new resident, how well you've taken care of it for me."

Lily evoked her inner Emma Stone and nodded, hoping her fake upbeat expression would come across passable. "Don't give me too much credit, Mama. I'm not like the hairstylist for the rich and famous or anything." These days, she'd be grateful if a poor and anonymous person stopped by for a cut.

Estelle held her hand. "No, but you're doing what you love and also keeping the business I created," she said, tears brimming in her eyes. Her mother rarely cried. "I just want to say, sweetie…thanks for all you've been doing. I worked hard to keep that place and made some of my best memories there."

A lump of frustration lodged in Lily's throat. She wanted to tell her mother the salon would be turned into a freaking parking garage, but the words got stuck in her mouth. She couldn't do that to her mother. Hell, she couldn't do that to herself. She fished out her cell phone from her pocket and glanced at the time on the screen.

Time to make up my mind.

• • •

"What do you mean, he's not available?" Lily asked after a woman with a clipped voice had picked up the cell phone number Marco had given her.

Shit. In less than forty minutes his offer would expire. Why was he playing hard to get now?

"Mr. Giordano is in a meeting. He asked me to tell you you're welcome to wait in his office," the lady with a British accent continued. "I'll give you directions to the VIP parking lot."

Lily barely registered the woman's instructions, but somehow, she managed to remember them half an hour later when she pulled into the garage. The Giordano Tower was an impressive building, and she had driven by it many times without knowing a thing about its owner.

She marched through the fancy lobby, and when she showed her ID, one of the clerks took her to the elevator himself. How confident was Marco that she'd accept his offer? Very. She doubted he'd set all this up if he thought she'd say no—she could decline over the phone. It'd have been easier. Cleaner.

Her heart thumped at each footstep she took once she exited the elevator on the top floor. She finally met the woman she'd talked to on the phone, Claire, an elegant lady in her fifties who kindly showed her in and offered her refreshments.

Alone in Marco's office, Lily skimmed the enemy's territory. A floor-to-ceiling glass wall brought in natural light and showcased Manhattan's financial district. An enormous leather chair, empty, and dark wood furniture screamed money. A couple of black sofas and several newspapers from different parts of the world were neatly stacked on the coffee table. To the right was a wet bar. She didn't miss a closed door, possibly a bathroom. This was the office of a man who moved millions every day. The office of a man who wanted to screw her for money.

Heat coiled low in her stomach, like a simmering fire waiting for the fuel to burst out in flames. A part of her hated him for thinking he could buy her, and another part of her hated herself for wanting to fuck him anyway.

When the door swung open, she spun on her heel in a mix of dread and anticipation. When this whole situation ended, she'd look for a counselor. There had to be a reasonable explanation for her crazy behavior.

"Lily." He locked the door behind him and walked to her with a wolfish grin.

She curled and uncurled her fists, worried her nerves would get the better of her. To get through this, she needed to exercise the self-control she didn't have. "Marco."

"I'm glad to see you. Please, have a seat," he said, pulling a chair for her.

She sat, and soon he made his way round the desk to sit in front of her. How did these negotiations take place? She decided on, "I have a counteroffer for you."

A slow smile curled at his lips.

She straightened her shoulders, proud of her external calm. "I'll be yours for a month. In return, you're paying all my debts *and* I'm keeping my beauty salon. I don't mind if you've already bought the other spaces around me, but you're not turning the strip mall into a fucking garage."

He pinched the bridge of his nose, letting out a sigh of annoyance. "Are we back to square one? How come your proposal gets you a lot more than before, and I don't get the valuable piece of property my company needs?"

Not my problem. "You're a resourceful man. If you look hard enough, you'll find another solution or another place nearby to ruin and get your goddamn garage," she said. If he said no and she lost her suite, she'd lose everything and be in debt for life. But she had to stand her ground and give her business a shot. If he wanted her bad enough, he'd do it.

"You're smart, and I appreciate your persistence. However, I need that space and you know it. Are you willing to lose my generous offer and the opportunity for us to fuck each other's brains out for a month?"

She stood, remembering what she had mentally rehearsed. Growing up, all her friends had been a lot more sexually aggressive and sassy than she'd ever been. She'd been a slow learner, a late bloomer, but at the same time, she'd heard a lot of stories on how to seduce a man. *I hope they're all handy now. Otherwise this is embarrassing.*

"You're missing the point. You'll be missing the chance to fuck me for a month," she said, and pulled her shirt over her head. She wished she had something sexier on, like hot pink lingerie and a suggestive trench coat. For now, her jeans and shirt had to do. "Do you know I haven't slept around a whole lot in my life? Had a couple of long relationships, but that's it," she said, staring at him square in the eye. She didn't miss the way his Adam's apple moved, like he'd swallowed hard. His gaze held hers, and a delicious strand of female empowerment traveled down her spine. "I never even tried anal sex. I suppose it can be fun with the right partner, but the pastor's daughter in me always thought that's too much of an indulgence to try with a man you're not married to."

He rocked back in his chair, shifted in his seat, and from where she stood she saw the hard-on burgeoning in his pants. "Keep talking."

"So I've never experienced butt play, or sex toys. Besides mediocre vaginal sex, I'm the next thing to a virgin." She unclasped the hook of her bra and let it fall off her arms to the floor. During high school, she'd tried to minimize her DD cups as much as possible, to keep from getting too much attention.

He licked his lips, and a charge of heat bolted down her core. Shit. She hoped she pulled this off. What if he threw his head back and laughed, kicked her ass so she'd leave crying with her clothes in her hands? "Wanna see something cute, Marco?"

He gave her a slow nod, his eyes darkening.

She pulled down the top of her hipster underwear, showing him the tattoo of a blue butterfly she'd gotten when she'd been seventeen. Her quiet, small act of rebellion. "I love butterflies, so I got this done. I guess it's the bad girl in me wanting to get out."

His gaze slid from her breasts down her belly until he saw the small tat under her waistline. "Take it off," he said gruffly.

She pulled up her underwear, hiding her butterfly from view. "See, I'd love to, but I can't. Not until I have your word."

With a sigh, he surged to his feet, thrusting his fingers into his hair. She didn't move an inch, resolute in not giving in. She'd thought this through during her drive from visiting her mother. If he'd wanted her badly enough, he'd go the extra mile. All or nothing.

"When we settle everything, I'll do my best to give you a worthy performance and take all my clothes off. Hell, I'll even dance for you. What is it going to be, Money Pants?"

Chapter Three

Marco thinned his lips to keep from saying yes.

Did she know how much of a hassle she'd created by refusing to sell them her space? Or hell, refusing to do what was best for her.

If they didn't make a deal, she'd lose her shop in a matter of weeks because of her mounting debts. He'd had a corporate investigator look into them—she had lost clients because a competitor opened across the street, but even before that her clientele had fled because she'd taken care of her father during his illness. Her mother had health problems herself, so Lily ended up taking care of both parents, thus not making enough money, and not showing up at work enough, canceling on clients.

She'd sacrificed for others, which was commendable and naive. He looked at her now, half naked in his office, and a rush of desire seared his veins. Her past and how many lovers she had before him didn't matter, but he believed her words. Despite the bold way she'd started her act, taking off her shirt and bra and almost sending him to the nearest ER with a heart attack, she wasn't a woman who did this every day. The challenge in her eyes had an undercurrent of fear, of vulnerability, probably because she questioned herself. Her beautiful hair stayed in a low ponytail when it should have been framing her striking face.

Lily's adorableness complicated things. She wasn't a sex toy, but a smart, kind, caring woman. The kind of girl one brings home to meet one's parents.

The kind of girl… An invisible light switched on inside his brain. His mind raced, a bolt of adrenaline rushing through him. Yes. How had he not figured this out before? After Elizabeth had declined his offer, he'd contemplated calling an actress, but even unknown actors had social media accounts and artists were, by nature, attention lovers. Meanwhile sweet Lily… "I'll meet all your conditions, if you agree to a small one of mine. Something new."

"What is it?" she asked, her voice unsteady.

He fixed his collar. Asking her to step in and pretend to be his fiancée seemed more preposterous than having her in his bed for a month. Of course, their chemistry resulted from an organic attraction, and there certainly wasn't anything organic about a pretend engagement. Hell, he'd had a short-lived, *real* engagement in the past, and that one didn't bring good memories, either. "In two weeks, I have a party to attend on an island in Italy. My grandmother is celebrating her last birthday," he said. Why beat around the bush, when Nonna's heart wouldn't see another year? From what he'd heard, she was still quite functional, even though her level of activity had decreased, and she had nurse technician who she introduced to friends as a simple companion.

She shrugged. "Oh. I'm sorry. Is this your way of telling me you want to use those days outside of the thirty days? Or does it mean I get a break from all the sex?"

"Means you're coming with me."

She blinked. Twice. "To Italy?"

"Yes. As my fake fiancée. I want to give my grandmother the gift of thinking I've...settled down. That's a parting present from me," he said after taking a deep breath.

She rubbed the back of her neck. "Wow. That seems a lot more complicated than being in a room with you."

"My family will adore you. All I ask is for you to remember this is just a farce," he said firmly. Not that he expected her to fall for him, but he needed to be honest about his intentions. His doomed relationship with Angelica had shown him he wasn't ready for marriage yet, or maybe ever. When that time arrived, he'd choose someone who was a good match in his life, using requirements that didn't include an untamable attraction. Excess of passion had been what ruined his parents' marriage, amongst other things, and he'd never subject himself or his future kids to the same fate.

"Oh, trust me, I'll know that every second."

He erased the distance between them and angled closer. "I hope not *every* second." He made an effort to keep his focus on her face and not slid his gaze down her soft neck and unbelievably full, large tits. His mouth watered at the sight of them, and he'd nibble and suck them in good time. Now they had logistics to worry about.

"So if I pretend to be your fiancée, you're all in? I get to keep my salon and you settle my debts?"

"Yes. Deal?" he asked, offering her his hand.

She glanced at his hand before stretching out her own for a handshake. "Deal."

He pulled her close until her naked body rubbed against his, and she gasped but didn't fight him. He inhaled her gorgeous fragrance and whispered in her ear, "I'll email you the contract in a couple of hours. Are you safe?"

"As in I won't steal your expensive watch when you're napping and sell it for cash?"

"Safe. Clean," he repeated, in a tone that left no room for misinterpretation.

"Yes, of course I am. I'm also on the pill. I did a routine check with my girl doctor last month, and if you want—"

"I believe you," he said. "I also saw a doctor recently, but I'm emailing you the results just so you know I'm telling the truth." He rarely embarked in an affair with a woman without using condoms. With Lily, though, he wanted nothing more than to be inside her completely. The idea stirred his groin. "Tonight, we'll go out and celebrate our agreement," he said, and couldn't resist lowering his hand down to her cute tattoo, slipping a finger inside her underwear.

She looked up at him, desire gleaming in her eyes. She shivered under his touch, a moan escaping from her sensual mouth. His whole being tingled, his body sending him signs of arousal he couldn't deny. *Dio*. He had to deny…for now. He couldn't take her yet—not without the confidentiality agreement in place, or the other contract he'd have his lawyer modify. "Get ready, gorgeous. Tonight, your butterfly will soar."

• • •

"Is she here?" Marco asked the hostess of one of the best restaurants in Manhattan. *Dio*, he hoped Lily liked sushi.

"Yes." Karen smiled. "She arrived twenty minutes ago, and we sat her at your favorite table."

He nodded. A habitué at the exquisite eatery, he knew exactly what that meant—the booth located on the second floor, in an intimate area. He strode through the soothing ambience formed by a miniature cherry blossom tree and several statues throughout the area. Low music played, more sounds than lyrics. He enjoyed coming to this place to relax after a long day.

Of course, he would have enjoyed it much more if he hadn't been late. His plan to pick her up, to make their deal a bit more personal, went down the drain when one of his properties had an accidental fire. No one had been hurt, but he had to make a statement, contact the PR team, and quickly visit the location to make sure everyone was safe. His brother was still in Los Angeles, and he decided to wait to tell him they weren't going to build the miraculous garage after all. Nico wouldn't be happy, but he'd deal.

When he arrived at the booth, a waiter was taking Lily's drink order. She smiled at the young man, and something inside him throbbed, like he could punch the guy for being the receiver of her radiant beam. One second in her company and he already wasn't thinking straight. That's why he needed to screw her until the novelty wore off.

"Hi," she said.

He noticed the hues of gold in her green irises, the freckles peppering her nose and cheeks. *Dio*, she looked even more delectable than earlier. Her blond hair was up, with a few strands framing her face. A cherry-red lipstick coated her kissable mouth, and a black dress clung to her curves. The U-neck cut displayed a generous amount of the valley between her breasts, her tits squeezed into the fabric.

A surge of arousal bolted through him. Without yanking his gaze from her, he slid next to her, grabbed the napkin, and placed it on his lap. "Hey."

"And for you, Mr. Giordano?" the waiter asked him.

"Scotch. On the rocks," he said, grateful he wasn't driving tonight. He'd entertained taking his own sports car and not using the limo service, but ended up deciding his hands should be on her at all times—certainly not on a steering wheel.

The waiter nodded and left.

"Sorry I'm late. I had to take care of something."

She waved him off. "It's okay. Like what you see?" she

asked him.

Shit. He'd been gawking at her, his mouth watering at her beauty like he was a horny teenager who never took girls out. Certainly not like the successful businessman who had no problem in finding a hot date. "You're wearing your hair up again. I was just thinking that's intriguing, given your occupation."

"Oh." She touched her hair, then her hand slid down her neck. "It's habit. I'm always doing stuff."

He scooted even closer to her. "May I?" he asked, resolute in letting her know that though he'd bought her body for a month, her wishes mattered. In fact, he craved to fulfill each one of them.

"Y-yes."

He touched behind her head, where a fancy pin held her hair together, then released it. Waves of sultry, silky hair fell down her shoulders like she'd stepped out of a shampoo commercial. His body rumbled, images of him taking her from behind and pulling her hair flooded his dirty mind. His cock strained against his slacks, and he mimicked her earlier move and let his hand glide down her neck. He felt her shiver at the contact and sighed.

"*Sei bellissima*," he said.

Her breasts rose and fell, her organic response to him cementing his decision. He wasn't the only one who needed this deal—she needed it just as much. If the contract gave him the go-ahead to indulge in her body without false promises, it probably also made her feel more comfortable with her sexuality, being a pastor's daughter and all. She knew—he hoped she did—he wouldn't judge her.

With that in mind, he drew an invisible, circular pattern at the base of her throat, feeling the pulse. She didn't tear her eyes from him, and her luscious lips parted, asking, no, begging to be kissed.

"Do you like sushi?" he whispered.

She leaned into his touch. "I can't stand it."

His heart skipped a beat. "Good. Let's get out of here."

. . .

Lily chewed on her lower lip. From the moment he'd given his hand to her until now, guiding her through the restaurant, her flesh had become überaware of Marco. He must have given someone a sign, as the limo stopped at the curb in front of them the second they hit the sidewalk. A movie scene wouldn't have had better timing.

When they entered the limo, the same luxury car that had picked her up at home and driven her here, Marco clicked the button to lift the partition.

"Sorry, sir, I meant to tell you there's something wrong with the button. I'll take it to the dealership tomorrow," the driver said, starting the engine.

Marco cursed in Italian under his breath and shot her a look filled with frustration. She chuckled, for she experienced that same crazy urge to get him naked and on top of her—or under her, or sideways.

She rested her hand on his knee, tapping it a couple of times in a silent message of comfort. He placed his hand over hers, and his warmth enveloped her skin. "Does the partition often break?" she murmured.

He smiled. "Never."

"Maybe it's a sign," she said playfully. "To take things slow."

Marco circled his index finger on her hand, the gentle and unassuming touch hardening her nipples. An unbearable ardor overpowered her, and she didn't need to touch her cheeks to feel their heat. She couldn't wait to have his long olive finger touching her intimately. A splash of apprehension blended with excitement. The driver was taking them to Marco's place.

The contract she signed earlier stipulated he wouldn't force her to do anything against her wishes. She'd be in his domain, though. What if he completely changed his mind and killed her? God, she really had to quit watching all those Lifetime movies.

"Where's the bold girl who stripped in my office earlier? The one who promised me a worthy performance?"

She had taken her clothes off because that had been part of a script she'd created. She'd had time, albeit brief, to think about a strategy to get his attention and get her way. And now...now she'd have to deliver the goods.

"Are you having buyer's remorse?" she asked, in another attempt to keep the mood light.

He lifted up her chin so she had no choice but to look deep into his eyes. "Never."

She half closed her eyes, tilting her head to the side and hoping he'd kiss her. But he stroked her jaw and stared at her without making any headway. "Why not?" she murmured.

He leaned down until his mouth brushed her earlobe. Tingles multiplied inside her, causing goose bumps to rise on her arms. "Because this is a new driver and I don't want pictures of me screwing the pastor's daughter online."

"Oh," she said, unable to hide her disappointment. "That'd be bad for your image."

"I'm more worried about your image." *Definitely.* How would she be able to pass as his lovely bride-to-be to his dying grandmother if pictures of her ass leaked all over social media?

Minutes dragged until they were finally driven into the underground garage of a high-rise building in Manhattan. He ushered her into an elevator, and just their luck, a couple of teenagers argued inside about a rock band's new song. Marco kept her close to him, his hand biting into her skin, and the nearness alone sent little thrills of excitement through her.

The elevator arrived at the top floor with a ping, and when they exited, she realized they were at the foyer of his penthouse. He snatched her to him, kissing her with such wild passion she almost fell back. She linked her arms around him and celebrated inwardly when he scooped her up. She'd appreciate the decor of his place later. Now she preferred to dive headfirst into this naughty ocean of sensations.

The one thing was obvious about his place—the size. By the time he eased her onto the mattress in his bedroom, her breaths came in small gasps. One more second and she'd be completely breathless. He began to undress, flinging his jacket across the floor without much fuss. When he pulled the shirt over his head, she sat. She'd felt his taut muscles, but now she saw them.

Her pussy clenched, the pearly cream filling her snatch. He caught her looking, and when he moved, the well-defined pecs and ridges of his six-pack bunched. Wow. This man… "It's like John Cena and Bruce Wayne had a son," she said, then realized she'd shared her nerdy comment out loud.

He grinned. "I've never been much of a Batman fan, but I'll take the compliment."

"If you're not a Batman fan, we may need to rethink all this," she said, circling her index finger.

"Don't worry, *tesoro mio*. I'll take you to Gotham City tonight," he said, and glided her on the bed until her feet touched the edge. He slid off her underwear, and she inhaled sharply. Within seconds, he disappeared between her legs, and she threw her head back.

This is really happening. She braced herself mentally that he'd second-guess, but nope. She watched him blow on the skin of her thigh, and resolution filled her.

He cupped her pussy, his hot breath causing tingles.

Moved by instinct, she squirmed, slightly swaying her thighs, but he hooked his hands under her ass and kept her in place. He licked her clit with the tip of his tongue, and she mewled, a strand of pleasure arrowing up and down her body. Whatever reason had brought them together, she wanted him—wanted this, and the degree to which she responded stunned her.

If he continued this way, she'd visit Gotham City a lot sooner than planned. He licked her folds and buried his head between her thighs. She thrust her hips into his mouth, and without delay he sucked her. A loud moan left her lips. She didn't mean to sound so dramatic, but there was only so much she could take. He thrust his tongue into her, his nose pressing into her twat.

She bucked, and soon spasms rode through her, and it took her a few seconds to catch her breath. "Holy Batman."

He licked every drop of her then worked his way up, giving her belly openmouthed kisses. She quivered, so soon, already recognizing that powerful craving fueling up inside her. He chuckled against her breasts, a hearty, manly sound. He knew exactly how much she needed him, and she couldn't save face. "You taste delicious," he said. "Wanna try?"

"Yes." *Yes, to everything*, a savage part of her shouted.

He dipped down and kissed her, his tongue bringing her own tangy essence to her palate. Tasting herself made her feel as primal as an exotic, foreign dance. She dove her fingers into his hair, pulling him closer, desperate for the warmth of their skin-to-skin contact. He broke the kiss, tracing down her neck, and she moaned.

"These are huge tits for a pastor's daughter," he said, cupping her breast.

"What are you going to do about it?"

He grinned. "I'm going to fuck them."

Chapter Four

Marco pulled her to the edge of the bed, then slid out of it himself. He wanted to play with her breasts, but it'd be easier if he didn't crush her with his weight. So, he positioned himself in front of her, and she took the hint, cupping her tits and pressing them together in an irresistible offer.

His blood rushed hot and thick to the tip of his cock, where pre-cum bubbled as his underside veins expanded. He wouldn't last long, but *merda*, he needed to last for her. Smiling, she loosened her grip on her tits, just so he could thrust his dick in between the fleshy mounds.

Oh, the sensations engulfing him… He could die now, with his cock nicely squeezed between her silky, firm tits, and he'd be absolutely okay with that. He stared at her, unwilling to jerk away his gaze. She was a showstopper. A blush covered her face, her eyes were semi-closed, yet she still managed to look at him as if she wanted to learn how to please him. He swallowed; his throat had never been this dry or thick. He moved his dick on her, heat radiating from her chest.

A groan or two escalated from the depth of his lungs.

Soon, she massaged her tits on him, the jism from his tip a natural moisturizer. He clasped her hands, showing her exactly how he liked her to touch him, guiding her. He increased the pressure, the rhythm, enjoying how her blush deepened but she kept looking at him, her eyes darkening to a Christmas-tree green.

"You know what? I want to taste you, too," she said, and before he replied, she'd palmed his rod and dipped down.

He threw his head back, his temples throbbing with excitement. She licked his length, her tongue lazily gliding on his cock. Meanwhile, she cupped his hard, heavy balls, putting just enough pressure to get him to growl.

"You're a naughty girl, aren't you? You like it dirty."

"I like it dirty with you," she said, then resumed provoking him, this time running the tip of her tongue along his rod.

Dio. She worked him to the point of no return. He was a breath away from coming, and the thought played in his mind. How delicious would it be to release himself inside her sinful mouth, while she kept her sexy eyes on his, swallowing every last drop of his seed? The image sent a spasm through him. He would fuck her mouth again and give her a good, hot load, but not this time. He touched her wrists, pulling her away from his rod, and said, "Get on your hands and knees."

"So bossy," she said, but did as told.

"Batman didn't get to where he was by being nice now, did he?"

"Point taken."

She splayed her hands and knees on the mattress.

"Lift your ass up."

She glanced over her shoulders. "You're out of control."

He brushed her belly, and she quivered, her back arching. What a sight. Sighing, he watched her for a moment in complete silence, tension stretching the air between them. He didn't want to ever forget this moment, even when she was long gone from his life. He hoped, even, that despite the unavoidable outcome at the end of their contract, he'd keep the sweet image of the gorgeous woman surrendering to him, with her delectable breasts bouncing down, her strawberry-shaped ass in the air.

Later, when the contract ended, she'd be indifferent to him, and maybe he'd feel the same way toward her. She might even foolishly try to get more out of him. Right now, he'd enjoy every second in her presence…every minute he'd bought.

"Is my ass so big you're changing your mind?" she asked in a light tone, yet he sensed nervousness in her voice.

"Your ass, like the rest of you, is overwhelmingly perfect," he said, nudging her thighs farther apart. "In the near future, I'll give it all the attention it deserves." The idea of plunging into her back entrance until he exploded teased him, but he knew he'd have to ease into that with Lily. He wanted to make it enjoyable for her, to have her rough moans filling the room.

Now, he'd focus on the wet, tight pussy he'd touched. He played with her folds just enough to confirm how much she wanted him to screw her. His gut clenched, his body throbbing for release. If he waited longer, he'd come in his hands.

He pulled her woman lips apart and plunged into her. She gasped, and for a moment her back arched, like she was getting used to having him inside her again. He took a sharp intake of breath, reveling in the exquisite sensation of her walls clinging to him without any barriers. Having sex without a condom wasn't something he did often, but with Lily… He had to give in to the raw need to claim her completely, free from any restraints. "Fuck, baby you're so tight. So tight and perfect. If I wasn't a second from coming, I'd suck your pussy all over again," he said truthfully. He'd loved her musky scent, the way her tender flesh responded to his tongue.

He leaned over her and searched for her clit.

"Oh, yes. Right there. Touch me, Marco."

Damn, he liked it when she called his name with such urgency. Her plea encouraged him to delay his own pleasure—as much as he could—and tease her, rubbing his thumb on the nub.

"So good," she said, breathless.

Now that she was distracted, he moved his rod inside her, earning another moan. He retreated, and when he thrust into her, he tapped her button with his finger, furthering the torment.

"This is… I feel so complete. Like you're inside all of me."

Her words pumped adrenaline into his bloodstream, dizzying his head for a moment. Complete. His heart skipped a beat. Damn it, that's how he felt, too. Like nothing else mattered as long as he buried himself inside her. *Snap out of it, man.* He blinked and continued the naughty dance in and out of her, gradually upping his rhythm. "One day, I'll fuck both your holes. I'll ram my cock into your gorgeous ass while working a vibrator into your greedy pussy," he said, needing the safety net of dirty talking.

"That sounds so good. But won't it hurt me?"

"I'll make sure you're more than ready when it happens. Will you let me, Lily? Will you let me fuck you any way I can?" he said, his body rigid with tension.

She rocked her hips into his cock. "Yes. God, yes. I'm coming from talking about it."

Strands of a powerful, exhilarating climax moved through him. Furiously. Madly. "I'm stuffing your cunt with my cum, baby," he said, breathing out. "All for you. Do you want it?"

"Yes. Yes, please. Oh, God," she said, and quivered, finding her own peak.

Driven to the brink, he let go, and his body shook as he exploded inside her. Joy stirred him, a powerful force that he had never experienced before. He slammed into her one last time, feeling every ounce of strength deserting him as he released himself deep inside her. That organic exchange, so simple and raw, caused him to smile.

Gradually, she lowered her body, and he realized he was too heavy for her, so he eased her onto the mattress and rolled to the side.

He ran his hand down his face. His heart carried on the frenetic beating for longer than he cared to count.

"I can't move. I'm destroyed," she said. "Can you wrap me in the sheet like a burrito and hand me to your driver?"

"What makes you think my driver is up this late?"

"Or request an Uber. That might be better. I need to hit a drive-through, anyway. I'm starving."

Starving. He slid out of bed and slipped on lounging pants. Then he walked around the bed. She remained still, with her ass in full view, her head to the side. Smiling, he wrapped the sheet around her.

"What, what are you doing?" she asked, her eyes reaching her hairline.

"I'm following your command, *tesoro*," he said, amusement dripping from his voice. If his employees, or hell, if his brother heard him talking this way, they'd deem him a lunatic. He lifted her from the bed, and she clutched the sheet to cover herself.

"I wasn't speaking literally. I can wear clothes before I leave."

He made his way out of his room, and only when he reached the kitchen did he put her on the stool at the marbled island. "There."

"Where's my ride?" she asked.

"Do you really think I'd let my driver or anyone else see you like this?" He bet the new guy would drool if he saw her so adorably bare. A possessiveness he wasn't used to—not when it came to women—poked him. Nonsense. Blaming it on his post-sex haze, he willed the sentiment away.

"Well, I don't want to overstay my welcome. The contract didn't specify sleepovers. I'm assuming that after the deed is done, you'll want me out of your hair. You know, to keep this real and not like the Shakespearean poems."

She had a point. Sleepovers could blur the lines quickly... Unless, of course, they did little sleeping. "I think there's a wide range between reality and love sonnets."

"True."

He kissed her nose then ran his finger along her cheek. "Besides, it's my duty to feed you. I helped you burn calories. Now let's replenish them."

. . .

Lily wrapped the sheet tighter around her. She sat on a tall stool in front of the large marbled island. "What do you have in that big, bad fridge?" she asked, pointing at the stainless-steel monstrosity with a built-in TV on the door. Everything in his kitchen was modern, white, and pristine.

He leaned onto the island, his fingers drumming the smooth surface. "What do you want?"

She cleared her throat. Her pussy still throbbed from the sex aftermath, a tingle filling her breasts. Maybe she should have taken an Uber and just left. Why did he waste time being nice to her? They'd had sex, and now they had nothing to talk about. Unless they screwed again. "If I say clam chowder or grits, is it going to magically appear before me?"

His lips broke into a smile that clawed its way into her heart and squeezed it. "I can have it delivered."

"I bet," she said, then chewed on her lip.

For a moment, they stared at each other without words to distract them. Ever since she was a kid, she'd always won stare wars because she managed to keep from laughing or blinking for the longest time. Her forgotten talent came in handy as she fought hard not to lean over the island and kiss him.

"I have an idea," he said, breaking contact first. "Are you allergic to seafood?"

She shook her head.

"Good. I'll make you one my specialties," he said, and turned around to fetch two pots from the cupboard.

She watched him get some organic, expensive-looking pasta from the pantry, as well as spices from the rack, and start working the stove. "Do you cook for all your, er, purchased lovers?" she asked, regretting her question the second it flew from her mouth. What else could she call herself?

He tossed her a glance over his shoulder then opened the freezer and produced a bag with precooked shrimp and scallops. Really, it shouldn't matter what he did with other women, anyway. A lot of guys were douches and pretended to be something they were not. At least with Marco, she knew what to expect from day one.

"I've had girlfriends before. You're my first purchased, temporary lover."

The confession brought a silly reassurance to her. She crossed her legs in a vain effort to keep her essence from seeping through the sheet and staining his stool. "Don't you say that to all of them?"

"No. I always put contracts in place, even with girlfriends, to protect my interests. But this is the first time I've signed a contract with much tighter clauses."

"So you don't pay your girlfriends for sex?" She admired the way his bare back glowed under the kitchen lights. His gorgeous, dark olive complexion enhanced the well-defined muscles and wide shoulders. Black lounging pants outlined his perfect ass.

"No."

"Then why contracts?" she asked, curious. It wasn't like he was marrying them and needed a prenup.

He continued to cook, but she didn't miss how his muscles tensed for a bit. He probably didn't get asked these things every day. Maybe she should leave this get-to-know-me question for later. Sure, they were hooking up, but did that mean she had to keep it super light all the time? Without giving in to curiosity?

"It's okay. You don't have to answer," she said. She didn't need to read a Booty Call 101 textbook to sense his uneasiness.

He shrugged and turned to her, peering at her with those gorgeous brown eyes yet still managing not to give away much. "Contracts help me keep things in perspective. I don't want to disappoint anyone who's thinking I'll give them what I'm not interested in giving. I don't lie, Lily. Besides, the confidentiality agreement ensures people won't be writing things about me, or posting on social media."

She drummed her fingers on the marbled counter. Behind all that overconfidence lurked the fear of compromising, which was even worse than commitment. At least in bed, she mused inwardly, Marco was a giver. "Isn't it boring, though? To know exactly how each of your relationships will evolve? Or in your case, not evolve?"

He opened a drawer and fetched silverware. "Contracts may be the same, but people aren't," he said, and continued to fumble with plates and other appliances. Her father always cleaned when issues at the church worried him, or he needed a breather. He hated cleaning, so whenever she or her mother found him wiping the kitchen countertops or dusting the shelves, they knew something bothered him.

"Truth. Why did you invite me to go on a trip and not one of your girlfriends?" she asked, her gaze following his movements even if he didn't stop to answer.

He grabbed the napkin holder and put it on the island. How many other objects would he move until she finished this conversation? "I did invite a girlfriend first. An ex. But she didn't take to the idea of pretending we were engaged after only dating for a few months."

"Oh. Do you miss her?"

"No," he said without hesitation.

The same way he won't miss me when I'm gone. "Because you don't get attached?"

He produced a wine bottle from the fridge and opened it. "Because I knew what to expect."

She toyed with the fork he'd arranged in front of her. "I guess I see a point. I always hope for the best and sometimes get kicked to the curb. I thought I'd be with my first boyfriend Harry forever. But after three years together, he slept with this girl from work."

"He was an idiot. But his loss is my gain," he said, filling two glasses of wine.

"That's right. A one-month gain," she said, emphasizing the amount of time they'd have together—if not to him, to herself.

He handed her a glass. "Cheers."

She enjoyed the straightforward light white wine with a fruity note. While he finished cooking the pasta, sautéing the shrimp and scallops in a sauce that teased her nostrils, she mused. Growing up, her parents always emphasized that sex was an act of love. Her father, more conservative, linked intercourse to marriage, family, commitment. Her mother thankfully, kept up with the times, but she still taught her one didn't screw another without special feelings involved. Certainly not for money.

They had a point, but why shouldn't she find out for herself? If anyone could teach her a thing or two about walking on the wild side, Marco Giordano fit the bill. Hell to the yes.

When he put a plate of angel hair pasta with shaved cheese and seafood in front of her, she breathed in the exquisite aroma. "This looks amazing."

He slid into the seat next to her, bringing his own plate. She never expected him to cook so well. She took bite after bite of the delicious dish, the spices and flavor scintillating in her mouth.

"It tastes amazing."

He angled close enough that his breath brushed her hair, sending a gazillion thrills through her. "So do you."

To dispel the tension, she twirled a good amount of angel hair onto her fork and brought it to her mouth. She didn't need to look at him to feel his gaze on her. She'd wrapped the sheet around her like a sarong, but now, as her chest rose and fell due to heavy breathing, the top suffocated her.

She clumsily tried to veer the conversation toward current events and politics, a subject certain to cool things down. They happened to agree on a lot of stances, and now she wished they didn't.

Finally, she dabbed her mouth on the napkin after finishing the food. She turned her face to him, glad to see him done as well. "Thanks for doing all this," she said, wondering if now would be a good time to put on her clothes and jet. She wanted to stay, but also had to be one step ahead of him to keep her feelings in check.

Marco's finger outlined the knot she'd made in the sheet. "You're welcome. How about some dessert?" he asked, undoing the knot, and soon, the sheet swooshed away from her, leaving her completely naked on the stool. Bare.

How in the world could she take a month of this without getting attached?

Chapter Five

Be ready at 5 p.m. I'll pick you up.

For the tenth time, Lily read the text message she had received earlier. She hadn't seen Marco in three days, ever since she'd slept over his place. He'd told her he'd had an emergency business trip to the West Coast, and she completely understood. A man like him, super busy and wealthy, had to prioritize his career.

Earlier that morning, she had just finished cutting an old client's hair when her phone buzzed. A silly rush of excitement had traveled through her, and it made waves every time she remembered she'd see him again.

She locked the shop's door and slipped her phone into her bag. She had vacuumed and cleaned up her apartment just in case he stopped by. Sure, they weren't in a legit relationship, but no reason not to tidy things up before a date. Or a meeting. Meeting was a safer word. A devil-dick appointment.

She could have waited for him inside the shop, but it was too soon to meet him there again. They'd already engaged in sex in the supply room. Though she'd agreed to the conditions of their contract, and she'd done more with him than any other man, she didn't want to make new memories with him in the place she'd keep forever. Letting go wasn't in her DNA, and dealing with the images of him screwing her in the supply room was enough.

Lily clutched her bag when she recognized him parking a Lamborghini in the lot. She drew in a breath and paced herself as she walked to him, to make sure he didn't know how much she'd missed his body on hers. Missed him as if he had come into her life a lot earlier than the few days prior. Missed him like someone who hadn't been fucked properly until she met Marco.

He slid out of his car and opened the door for her. Dark denim jeans and a black long-sleeved shirt covered his sinfully sexy body. When she was within a few inches of him, she balked, unsure if she should shake his hand, kiss his mouth, or compromise with a hug. Her pulse fluttered at any of those options, and the idea of touching him sent a ball of heat rolling through her.

"*Ciao.*" He closed the distance between them and deposited a kiss on her cheek. She parted her lips when he brushed his own on her flesh, needing so much more. The tips of her breasts throbbed, seeking a relief only he'd bring. "How've you been?"

"Good. How was your trip?" she asked, and slid inside the car, the buttery leather seat caressing her skin. A heat moved through her chest, his nearness enough to tease the little hairs at the back of her neck.

"Longer than expected," he said, and started the engine.

She worried her bottom lip to keep from babbling. He didn't pay for an emotionally needy woman or for the girlfriend experience. He wanted good fucks without the baggage. In silence, she mused over those things again, despite the bargain she'd agreed to with him. She looked out the window, thankful for the hustle and bustle of everyday life distracting her from their non-conversation in the car.

"You have your hair down," he said. "Looks nice."

Driven by instinct, she touched the ends of her hair, which she had styled with the curling iron earlier. She didn't mean to look like a freaking Disney princess, but ended up overdoing it. "I like to try new styles."

"I'm all for trying new things," he said smoothly.

God. Her nipples tingled, her breasts feeling heavy and full. What the hell did that mean? They hadn't tried anything she didn't enjoy, but what if he took her to an orgy? What if he got his rocks off by watching her with another man?

He drove by busy streets downtown, then a number of restaurants and clubs. When the car entered a parking garage, she decided it was time to know his plan. "Where are we going?"

"You know how you stripped for me in my office and teased me about giving me a worthy performance? You said you'd even dance for me."

She cleared her throat. *Sweet lord.* Why had she said those things? "Yes."

"Now we're going all the way." Marco parked the car, then slid out and opened her door. "It's a strip club," he said, grinning.

She withdrew. "Say what?" She'd never been to one but had seen them in the movies, and she'd heard stories. If he expected her to undress in front of a bunch of strangers, he'd better think again. No amount of money or family legacy would be enough for her to shred the last sliver of decency she had.

He took her hand in his and gave her a light squeeze. "It's not what you're thinking. They also rent individual rooms. You'll have your own pole, and I'll be the only one watching."

Oh. "Why didn't we do this back at your home?"

"Because I fantasized about you taking your clothes

off for me, rubbing yourself on a pole… Teasing me while I watch and stroke my cock."

Her clit throbbed, her walls drenching. "That's a nice image." She only hoped she could deliver. Her father always condemned tight or skimpy attire. She'd once been asked to try out for her high school's cheerleader squad, but declined without even checking with Dad. Why waste her time?

A large security man opened the door for them. The interior reminded her of a nightclub, with a few recessed lights shining down on the otherwise dark space. A blond woman dressed in a cherry-red minidress walked up to her with a key in her hand.

"Hi." She gave a small smile, looking at Lily. "I'm Dusty. You'll come with me," she said, then gave Marco the key. "Make a left and enter the first room."

Dusty made a gesture for Lily to follow her, and she did, after sharing a sideways glance with Marco. He didn't seem fazed by the rules. Had he been here before? Her stomach tightened.

Dusty strode with intent, making Lily straighten her shoulders and try to keep up the pace as they turned into a long hallway. A burgundy-colored carpet led the way, and on both sides there were doors, all of them closed.

Lily expected to hear music, or people talking, yet she heard nothing. Tension built in her core, fast-tracking her cells, making her hot and bothered. Finally, Dusty came to a halt in front of the last room and opened the door. Sucking in a breath, Lily entered to find an area about the size of her salon, filled with packed shelves, a collection of hats, and numerous glitzy costumes hanging on the rack.

A round, oversize mirror hung on the light purple wall, in front of a white vanity table. A wide range of curling irons, makeup items and—wait, was that body glitter?—crowded the surface.

Dusty folded her arms, tapping the toe of her high heels on the floor. "Are we ready?"

Was she? Apprehension clogged her throat, and she had to swallow to speak. "This is my first visit. What's the deal?"

"You can pick whatever costume or pieces of clothing you want to wear. Your boyfriend bought the platinum package, so you get to keep them, too. Then, feel free to use what you need to play the part. When you're ready, open that door," Dusty said, pointing at a door on the opposite side of the room. "He'll be waiting for you on the other side. It's a soundproof room."

Soundproof. The word rang in her head. A pang of relief loosened her limbs. At least no one would overhear them if, well, things escalated. She assumed if she stripped for him, he wouldn't let her leave with just a smile and a handshake.

"Do you have any questions?" Dusty asked.

"No." Of course, she had tons of questions, but obviously not enough time to ask them.

Dusty nodded. "You have a good body and a nice pair of tits. When you're done with him, consider coming back. We have a few regular strippers. They make a lot of money."

"Thanks," she said, making an effort to smile. The thought of any man's eyes or hands on her other than Marco's didn't appeal to her one bit.

Dusty left, closing the door behind her.

Lily approached the rack and skimmed the clothes, sliding her fingers on the material—some felt scratchy to the touch, like cheap Halloween getups. Others were silkier and softer. Each costume looked new or recently dry-cleaned. She picked the cheerleader one, chuckling. She searched for a Cat Woman or Harley Quinn outfit but didn't find either.

Gosh, she'd be here forever. She went through the other ones: the dominatrix, the vampire, the schoolgirl, the devil, the angel, the Playboy Bunny. She snorted. Not in this world would she squeeze herself into that glorified Spanx.

A baby-blue outfit got her attention. Labeled on the tag as "Sexy Nymph," it consisted of a cropped top with a golden trim, and a miniskirt in the same colors, with a sparkly sheer fabric in addition to the skirt. That's how Marco made her feel—like a Sexy Nymph.

She could choose something outrageous like Lady Gaga, but she preferred to be someone closer to herself, someone he, devil that he was, had created, or at least triggered.

Squealing with excitement, she removed her clothes and folded them into a pile. She kept her G-string and bra, slid the top over her, then pulled on the skirt.

One look at the round mirror confirmed she'd made the right choice. While she wouldn't be caught dead wearing this ensemble in public—unless she wanted to be arrested—it certainly worked for what she had in mind.

She clasped the doorknob and twisted it. Her heart raced wildly when she stepped into the mysterious place. A sexy song caught her attention. "Slow Hands" by Niall Horan. A few different rays of colored light moved inside, all focused on the center stage. This room seemed a bit bigger than the one she'd just left, but still quite intimate. Even though a few chairs occupied the area under the podium, only one of them was occupied.

Her pulse skittered.

Marco sat in the chair like he owned the place. He shot her a look filled with desire and awe. She sashayed toward the small stage, keeping her gaze locked with his. A hot stirring shook her, and if she had no willpower, she'd run to him now and fuck him right away. But this little game turned out to be a great lesson for self-control.

She slid her hand on the metal pole, the surface clean and shiny. She fisted it, like she wanted to do to his cock, moving up and down. It became hard to command her body to dance and make strategic movements when her insides roared for the man grinning at her. The man who had bought her.

• • •

I'm a bastard.

Marco shouldn't have brought Lily to this place, but hell, that made him a lucky bastard. He rocked back in his chair, fidgeting to keep from slapping out his dick and punishing it in front of her while he watched her dance.

He had no idea what her costume was—didn't matter. It could be an angel without wings, or a slutty Renaissance homage. The blue brought out her sparkling eyes, and the way the clothes fit her body drove him over the edge. Then she began to move, curling her leg around the pole, her delectable ass wiggling in tune with the song, and his cock strained in his pants.

Dio. This woman was the sexiest, most fuckable one he'd ever met. Maybe she read his thoughts, or simply peered at his painful erection, for she added some pep to her dance, caressing her top. His gut clenched, and a bolt of lust pounded his veins.

"Take it off," he said curtly, disappointed by his lack of discipline. This should also be about giving her some control, showing her how hot she was, and how she should be proud of every inch of her body.

She licked her lips seductively and writhed her hips against the pole, undulating them from side to side as she slowly slid down the length to the floor. "You're in a hurry, aren't you, big boy? But you'll have to wait for everything you want to see, to touch, to fuck."

He cleared his throat. He almost parted his lips to apologize, but his desire for her upped his internal temperature so badly, he was afraid he'd just growl. Lily Jenkins brought out the caveman in him.

"I'll give you a little something," she said, then took off the top.

He wished she'd gotten rid of her bra, too, but the piece of lingerie barely contained her perfect breasts. She cupped them, pinching her nipples until they pebbled against the silky fabric, moaning. Oh, yes. He liked seeing her pleasure herself, touch herself as if he were doing it to her.

She twirled around the pole, gaining more familiarity. He loved how her tits shifted every time she moved. Red stained her cheeks, making him wonder if she was feeling shy or if the sensual dance turned her on. By the way she moved and moaned, he'd bet she was as hot and bothered for him as he was for her. He preferred assuming she was hot for him, too.

Oxygen nearly vanished from his brain. He needed some relief, otherwise he'd come in his damn pants. He unbuckled his belt and undid his zipper. He had gone commando to make things easier.

He took his hard cock in his hand and stroked it. "Keep taking them off."

She peeled off her skirt, then her bra. All she had on was a sinful, sheer G-string.

She teased him, sliding her fingers into her underwear then removing them. Like a little devil, she lowered the thin side of the G-string, winked at him seductively, then lifted it again, continuing her sassy routine.

A dizzying sensation made him bob his head, as if he'd just been clocked. He blinked, determined to stay in the moment with the woman who socked air from his lungs. He'd visited enough strip clubs in his wild days to know Lily didn't have the moves of a professional, which only made her more endearing. She could have said no, or straight-up screwed him on the spot, but she played along, moving that sensual body just for him.

She popped her ass to the side, nearly giving him a cardiac arrest. He upped the rhythm of his strokes, pumping his cock, knowing too damn well he wouldn't make it long. She wiggled out of her G-string at long last and flung it in his direction. He grabbed it from the air, catching a whiff of her lovely, tangy, female scent.

For a moment, she stopped, watching him. "Don't you need a hand?"

"I don't want to make this about me," he hissed out. "I just need some release before I feast on you."

She gestured to the stage. "Come here."

What did she propose? Didn't she know if she sucked him or touched him, he'd come instantly? Still, he went to her, though it took every ounce of concentration to erase the distance between them.

Because of her heels and the advantage of the stage, she was almost as tall as he. He dipped his head only a little. "What do you want?"

"I want you to come on me again."

His temples throbbed. Anticipation rushed through him, desire dotting his vision. "You're a dirty girl, Lily."

She shot him the mischievous smile of a college student rather than a stripper. Then, she kneeled before him. Upon the sight of such a gorgeous woman, giving herself to him so openly… He came undone, a loud groan slicing the air. He pointed his dick at her epic tits, and soon his hot load hit them, and she didn't even blink. She massaged her breasts, encouraging him for more, and he shot his entire fill on her.

Holy fuck. It took several seconds for his breath to calm down, for the throb in his knees and his heart to subside. She took a sample of his cum from her nipple and brought it to her mouth, painting her lips with it and licking them. "Nice," she said.

His white cum dripped down her tits and onto her belly, and she had never looked lovelier. He'd branded her, in one of the most visceral, primal ways a man could a woman. Sure, there were other ways he wanted to try, too… But all in good time.

"You're a sex goddess, Lily Jenkins."

She licked the corner of her lips again. "Actually, I'm a sex nymph. That's what my costume label said."

"Suits you. Now lay on your back my dirty nymph, because I'm going to eat your pussy until you come in my mouth."

The glint in her eyes made him want to stroke her cheek for an endless amount of time. "I love when you talk that way."

"I know you do, because you are, in fact, a nymph. A woman who deserves to be thoroughly pleasured," he said, thinking how much he'd missed her the last three days. He'd thought this trip to California would be for just a few hours, otherwise he'd have asked her to go with him.

She lay down on the stage, and he scooted her to the edge so her screw-me shoes lay on his shoulders. Without delay, he dipped his head and blew some air on her sex. He knew the act would enhance her awareness. He got his response when she squirmed, and erotic moans filled the air.

"Yes. Oh, yes. Marco..."

Encouraged, he outlined her clit with his tongue, teasing her, wanting her to explode. She thrust her hands in his hair, shoving his face deeper into her, showing him how she wanted it.

"Eat me. I want you to eat me so bad, babe. I love how you fuck me with your tongue."

He thrust his tongue in her pussy and hooked his hands under her butt cheeks to lift her up and improve his angle. He loved tasting her, being pressed against her warm, sticky thighs. She was so wet... He lapped it up, each time driving his face deeper into her cunt, his nose pressing against her. She clenched her legs around his neck, and he knew she had to be getting close.

Relentlessly, he teased her, alternating between licks to her pussy and kisses on her swollen clit. Soon, she bucked toward him and called out his name, coming undone in his mouth. He feasted on her every drip of her delicious, pearly essence.

When her legs loosened around him and he lifted his head, he realized his own body had begun to reignite, the throbbing in his core making him harden again.

"When all this is over, I'll miss you," she said, looking at the ceiling, her voice soft.

Me, too. The words never ripped from his throat. Admitting them would make him vulnerable to her, and what if she used it as leverage against him later? Just because Lily seemingly had a good heart didn't mean she wouldn't use his feelings against him in the future.

He sat on the stage and brought her to his lap. The song still played somewhere in the background, and those annoying lights rhythmically pulsed rays of blue, pink, and yellow onto their skin as they strobed throughout the room. She arranged herself on top of him, straddling him. His cum still slicked her skin, but she didn't care, rubbing it on herself. She glanced at him with interest, her gorgeous eyes gleaming with challenge. What did she expect him to say?

His heart squeezed as if she had wrapped a vise around it. A part of him sent out a warning signal, for him to get her out of his life, quickly. Yet the side of him he feared, the one he found hard to control whenever he was next to her, disagreed.

He found himself thrusting his fingers into her sultry hair and pulling her into a kiss that ended one torture and started a much bigger one. She tormented him with her tongue, grazing her teeth on his upper lip. He slid his hand down her ass, positioning her at the perfect angle for screwing.

She reached for his buttons, undoing them without finesse. A couple of them flung in the air as she pulled his shirt down, probably needing the intimate contact, and raked her nails down his back.

His breath caught in his throat. He pulled her closer, his chest rubbing on hers. Her warm skin made his chest hair stand on end, a bombastic energy passing between them. *I'll miss you, too.* He silenced the words again with a hot, passionate kiss, and guided the small of her back with his hand until she sat on his cock. Oh, the glorious feel of having her walls tightly squeezing him. She must have felt it, too, for she threw her head back and gasped. This position allowed him to go deep into her, so deep. "Look at me, Lily. Let's get there together."

She leaned into him and rocked her head forward in a nod. "Yes."

He pressed her lower back harder, helping dictate the rhythm of their sensual dance. She followed his lead but soon started her own pace, and he obliged, loving the sight of her moving on him. She leaned into him and bit his shoulder, her teeth digging into his skin. Ache and excitement speared inside him, and he urged her on with his body, wanting it to last forever.

She rode him, rocking her hips backward then forward, taking all of his rod only to retreat a little. Moans flew from her full lips, and she teased him with that dangerous game until he saw the pulse beat at her neck, her cheeks flush, and her body shake. She was coming on his cock, and he finally let go, released himself so he'd reach the apex at the same time she did.

He stretched out his arm and caught her hand in his. Their fingers intertwined, palm against palm. She contracted her inner muscles one last time, until a sexy cry warned him. When he let go, his body convulsed, and he reveled in letting his hot cum into her tight pussy. All of it. All for her.

Chapter Six

"Hey," Nico said, striding into Marco's office without being announced. Nico had been alive three years longer than Marco, but sometimes the impatient and bossy way he acted made it seem like he had a whole decade on his brother.

Marco, however, had no problem putting Nico in his place. He raised his gaze from the paperwork he was signing and rocked back in his chair. "How was Los Angeles?"

Nico sat in front of him. "Good."

"How's Zaine doing? I haven't seen him in a while," Marco said, mentioning Nico's buddy from college. These days, Nico juggled business on both coasts, and whenever he visited California, he visited Zaine Cavanaugh and his wife Ashley.

Nico scratched his chin. "Okay. Doesn't seem like his marriage will hold up."

"Really?"

"Yeah."

"I'm surprised. They seem like a good match," Marco said, remembering the way the power couple completed each other.

"You and your matches. By the way, where's Elizabeth? Haven't heard much about her lately."

He shrugged. "I don't see her anymore." He didn't miss Elizabeth one bit. Ever since his return from his business trip a few days prior, whenever he was away from Lily, he'd counted the minutes until they were together again. The image of Lily's radiant smile flooded his mind, and need drilled through his body. The day before, he'd taken her shopping and provided her with all the best dresses and shoes money could buy. He couldn't wait to—

"You're smiling like a fool. Who's the new lady?" Nico asked.

The one keeping us from getting the garage. "She's someone I enjoy being around. She's…not like others."

"Other women?" Nico drew his eyebrows together.

His brother had never been much of a romantic himself, preferring a string of casual relationships to settling down. He'd even mentioned a couple of times he wanted to get a vasectomy. Marco would brush the subject aside, not really believing his brother would see that plan through.

"Other people. Anyway, there's something more important I need to tell you. We'll have to find another garage for the new entertainment district."

Nico rocked his head back, then threw it forward, sighing. "We've already exhausted all the options. The next site for making a garage is a few blocks from most restaurants and places. What's the holdup? I thought you wanted to talk to the beauty shop owner."

"I have, and she's adamant on keeping it."

"Didn't the corporate investigator look into her situation? Isn't she financially strapped?"

"Yes."

"I wonder if it's just a matter of time. But I gotta say, we can't wait long. The investors won't be happy about it, and some may even back out. Besides, I want to get on Brad Franklin's good side. I heard he's been doing a lot of business with Antoine Desmarais."

"So?"

"So, Desmarais owns that property in Mauritius I've been dying to buy since our father sold it."

Marco threw his hands in the air. When would his brother give up on this ridiculous dream of buying their childhood vacation home? Whatever feeling Nico expected to revive when he entered the place where—according to him—they were happy, it wouldn't happen. Desmarais, the owner, was extremely reclusive and had been for years. He'd lived in the home full time and had turned down every chance of selling it, despite the high purchase prices his brother had offered. "You need a new obsession, man."

"Maybe I'll call Elizabeth now that you're out of the picture," Nico said, obviously to tease him. They had better bro code than that.

"Be my guest."

"*Porca miseria*, Marco. You can't be this nonchalant about losing a deal because of a fucking beauty shop. If our father heard you, he'd—"

"What? He'd tell me I'm no good for anything? We're dealing with someone's livelihood here, Nico. It's her choice. She doesn't want to lose the salon. We can't make her give up her dream. We're rich, not mind manipulators."

Nico squinted his eyes. "I'll give it more time. Jerry said within weeks she should lose everything. But once that happens, that's it. We're taking over, whether we buy it from her or the bank seizes it from her."

Marco pondered. He had no problem telling his brother about his one-month arrangement. Nico was no saint, and didn't often judge another's sexual debauchery. But, if he told him, Nico would criticize his mixing business with pleasure in a way that could alter lives and a huge business deal. Nico would make a big deal out of everything. After the month ended, Marco would tell his brother about the deal and tell him to fuck off. Until then, he planned on enjoying Lily, guilt-free. Worry-free.

• • •

Hours later, he picked Lily up in front of her salon. They only had an hour or so before they had to endure the nasty traffic to get to the private airfield and take off for Italy and a week of celebrating Nonna's birthday.

"Are you ready to start your fake fiancée duties?" he asked, picking up her luggage, adamant on reminding her about the role she'd be playing abroad.

"Yes." She had insisted on meeting him at the salon and not in her apartment because of a client's appointment for highlights. Her work ethics pleased him. She didn't see all he could do for her professionally. She still counted every and each client—scattered as they were—as important as luxurious international travel. He doubted she'd done much of that.

He put her bags into the limo, even though his driver would have been happy to do so. When he opened the door for her, she slid inside, and he followed.

"I see the partition has been fixed."

He groaned. "Come here."

She sat on his lap, and their bodies molded together as if a skilled artist had created them. Warmth enveloped him, her feminine scent teasing his nostrils. She ran her fingers through his hair, transforming his scalp into a profusion of sensations. He leaned into her touch, enjoying it, afraid he'd gotten too used to having her near.

He slid his hand down her jeans. Ah, he hated when she wore jeans or any other piece of clothing where instant fucking became a difficult task. "I thought I told you not to wear pants."

She planted small kisses around his mouth, cheeks, and chin. By now, she should know that strategy drove him crazy, making him desperate to have her lips on his. "Yes, and I thought I told you we aren't living in the fifties anymore."

He swatted her ass playfully. "*Scopa*," he cursed.

She nibbled his nose and adjusted herself on him so she straddled him. "Say that again."

"You don't know what I said."

She chuckled. "Sounds sexy."

"You know what's sexy?"

She shook her head.

He pulled her head back to really take in her face, her lovely features. He caressed her cheek with his other hand, reveling in the intensity her big green eyes threw at him. "You are..." he said hoarsely, and brought her mouth close to his. "Sexy...and a whole lot of trouble."

• • •

"I still can't believe you didn't wake me up," Lily said in the limo that drove them from the airfield in Rome. He'd actually let her sleep the entire flight, when she should have enjoyed all the amenities.

"You seemed tired."

Sure, the chair converted into a bed, and the fluffy blanket had been a decadent invitation to Snoozeville, but... "I know, but what are the chances of me flying internationally in a private plane again?" Or hell, flying internationally anywhere?

"You still have the return trip to the United States," he

said drily.

"That's true. I'll make sure I won't sleep then."

Now he sat across from her in the sophisticated vehicle that had been waiting for them. Their surroundings were still foggy, but she kept her eyes glued to the window in case the scenery changed.

"We need to talk," he said, sounding more stern than usual, for the second time since they'd landed.

"Yeah?" she asked, without looking at him.

"Lily." He called her with an edge of impatience in his voice.

She regarded him. "What is it?"

How come he still managed to look that hot so early in the morning? She had brushed her teeth and combed her fingers through her hair, but Marco Giordano could easily make the cover of People's Sexiest Man Alive edition without even trying.

"We need a new name for you while you're here. I can't call you Lily to my family. My brother will be present, too, and he'll be suspicious if I introduce you as my bride and your name is on the deed of the salon we're trying to buy."

She pinched her skin at her throat, desperate to fidget away her worry. "What do you mean, trying? We have a deal. There's no buying."

"I know. I didn't want to break the news to my brother, Nico, who's my partner in this district revitalization. Not just yet."

"Why not?" she asked, her heart racing. This didn't sound good. Sure, he had paid off half of her debts—and the other half he'd pay at the end of the month, as agreed. What if Marco changed his mind? What if his brother convinced him that the fiancée facade wasn't worth the millions of dollars they'd lose from not having that garage?

"Lily, that's between me and my brother. You don't

have to worry about it. I gave you my word, and we signed a contract."

"Yes, but as far as I know, you can hire a lawyer with some top legalese bullshit and screw me in the end."

"That's not what I promised."

"Do you always fulfill your promises, Marco?"

He glanced away for a heartbeat, and when his gaze found hers again, she didn't miss the speck of bitterness in his dark amber eyes. And maybe…regret? "I'll fulfill this one," he said. "As I was saying, it'll be best to call you a different name."

"Patricia," she said. When she was a little girl, she always named her dolls Patricia after a kindergarten friend who had been far better off than her. "Sounds like a name of someone with money. Because that's what the fancy clothes you bought me are about, right? I'm assuming you won't tell them I'm a hairdresser, either," she said, proud of herself for not sounding whiny or defensive.

Her insides knotted. She had a lot of pride in her occupation, and in how much her mother had sacrificed to own her salon. However, in a world of wealth such as Marco's, she was a menial worker who offered services. She wasn't a doctor, lawyer, or a CEO.

"We can say you work with investments. It's broad enough."

"Sounds good." She forced a smile. "Anything else? Maybe some Ivy League university and a fancy fundraising hobby?"

"You don't have to sound so offended. I'm being practical. Hiding your real identity will be less of a headache for everyone. Including you."

She sighed. She guessed she didn't need his seemingly overbearing brother on her ass. Besides, wasn't this why she had accepted the contract—to pretend to be his fiancée?

Don't get it twisted. Despite the off-the-charts hot sex also included in their month-long agreement, Marco didn't need her for anything else. Chances were, if he ever married, he'd go with one of those types, someone more like himself.

Finally, the drive became a lot more interesting. She ignored him completely, fascinated by the life unraveling in front of her. The car wound through busy streets, where people walked their dogs and locals drank at the cafés lining the streets. When the scenery became posher, with a handful of luxury storefronts from designer brands she'd only heard about, the car slowed down.

"Are we close to your place?" she asked, imagining his place would be a lot more sophisticated than a simple walk-up apartment. Most likely he owned a swanky loft or luxurious penthouse.

"We're going to a jewelry store," he said.

Oh, yeah. The engagement ring. She assumed he'd borrow one, like those celebrities at high-profile red-carpet events, though a man of his means probably didn't rent anything. Maybe he'd exchange it afterward.

"Do they open this early?"

"I called the manager and asked them to open for me. I thought it'd be more practical to get it out of the way. Besides, there are no paparazzi this early. I'd hate for the news to reach my grandmother before I tell her myself."

"Sure."

The driver stopped in front of the store, and as usual, Marco slid out first and helped her out, stretching his hand for her. She could get used to the touch of his manly, strong, tanned fingers on hers. But she shouldn't—they'd only be together two more weeks, and then they'd go their separate ways.

He touched the small of her back, guiding her through the jewelry store.

A tall brunette with gorgeous cobalt eyes greeted them. She looked like she could rock a catwalk, making Lily feel ridiculously out of place. "Mr. Giordano, what a pleasure. We've put aside some engagement rings for you two to look at," she said in accented English, then nodded at Lily. "I'm Stefania."

"Nice to meet you."

"*Con piacere*. Please, have a seat."

For the next few minutes, she measured her annular finger, and another terrifyingly good-looking woman who could be on the cover of *Shape* magazine brought a velvet case. When she opened it, Lily's jaw dropped.

Several rings greeted her—most of them with huge diamond rocks. One of them seemed to be ruby, and a stone whose name she didn't even know. Marco murmured a couple of words of encouragement for her to try them on, but she felt a thread of panic float up her throat.

When she'd said yes to this whole farce, she hadn't envisioned the amount of times she'd be lying—to his family and friends, to salespeople and whoever crossed their path. Would she lie to herself, too? Had she?

She glanced down at the exquisite ring that Marco slid on her finger. It weighed heavy on her, and it meant nothing.

"What about this one?" he asked her, nudging her elbow.

She removed the ring from her finger as if it burned her, and put it on the glass table. "I…need some air. I'm sorry," she said, and surged to her feet. Without looking back, she left the store.

• • •

Fucking great. "I'll be right back," Marco said to the saleswoman, and stood.

Why did Lily run away? Buying jewelry shouldn't have

this effect on her, especially when he'd told her what they were about to do. In fact, she signed a piece of paper, a contract, agreeing to be his temporary fiancée. What had changed?

His heart squeezed, like a grand piano had fallen on him. Like those silly cartoons he and his brother watched when they were kids—their nannies always indulged them with excessive TV time. With a dry throat, he followed her steps, knowing it took him half as many to catch up to Lily outside the shop.

It was too damn late for her to change her mind. Unless she had looked at the ring and gotten some ideas. "You can't raise the price of our bargain, if that's what you're thinking about," he said, pretty sure she could hear him.

She turned around, the early morning wind playing with the tips of her hair. Her eyes seemed glossy, but she didn't let a tear roll down her cheek. "It's all about money for you."

"This has been about a lot more than money. It has been about making an old lady happy, and you keeping your salon. Is there money involved so those two things can happen? You bet. But they're happening for other reasons."

She tilted her head as if pondering on his words. "Then why did you just treat me like a cheap hooker, assuming I'd demand more money for my services?"

He ran his fingers down his face. *Because I'm an asshole.* "I'm sorry, Lily. I've visited a jewelry store once before with the intention of buying a ring for someone," he said, remembering that day several years ago, when he'd taken Angelica to a store as luxurious as the one they'd just walked from.

"Oh. I didn't know you were engaged before."

"It never happened. She called it off before we broke the news," he said, proud that he'd kept the bitterness out of his voice. "We weren't a match."

"And she couldn't have told you that when she said yes?"

"It's in the past. It would have been a stupid mistake." He'd shared things with Angelica he had always feared people would learn about his past. He'd trusted her, and her gentle and sweet way, but after knowing more about the man she'd agreed to marry, she decided to call it off.

Frustration formed a lump in his throat. He'd been fool enough to think he could be with someone like Angelica… uncomplicated and genuine. Or maybe he could have, if only he had kept the most private parts of his past, of his childhood, to himself. No one needed a traumatized child with abandonment issues. Not even him. He'd said goodbye to that part of him a long time ago. He'd never be the kind of husband she needed or deserved.

"Why did you run out?" he asked, to deflect her attention from him. He sucked in his breath, hoping to God she wouldn't change his mind so late in the game.

"I… I felt strange. I'm sorry if I triggered any bad memories for you."

"You're fine. Listen, I understand this is all probably overwhelming to you. What we tell my family about the nature of our relationship is a lie, but I enjoy being with you. That's real. That's all I can give you, but it's still real," he said. Fuck, he didn't want her to think he'd do this with anyone else. If he had hired an actress, he certainly wouldn't screw her.

"Why did your former fiancée break up with you? Did you cheat on her?"

"No cheating."

She frowned. "What did she find out, then? It's a big change of heart."

"She found out I'm not the type who hosts a family Sunday lunch. That I'm one of the reasons my father drinks like there's no tomorrow. That I'm not husband material if you want the fairy-tale kind of marriage."

She drew back, her face creasing, probably because she tried to digest all the words he vomited at her.

"What do you mean your father drinks because of you? No one does that."

He let out an exasperated sigh. She didn't quit, did she? The last thing he needed was for her to pity him, or to start some psycho-babble about his feelings. She was the woman he was supposed to screw, enjoy, and laugh with. If he turned what they had between them into more than that, he'd regret his decision. "I'm done talking about this subject. Are we doing this or not?" He tilted his head in the direction of the shop's front door.

Chapter Seven

"Need help?" Marco asked, nibbling her neck.

Lily struggled to speak—didn't really want to. Tingles spread the second he lowered her fluffy white robe. After they'd selected an engagement ring, they had spent the day sightseeing, eaten at a famous restaurant in the evening, and she had taken a hot shower in his luxurious bathroom.

God, how she wanted him. They hadn't screwed since their arrival in Rome earlier that day. She'd appreciated that he made it a priority to show her the sights on the only day they had before proceeding to the town by Lake Como where his grandmother lived.

He cupped her breasts. She let her head fall back and enjoyed how he dipped his head, his breath fanning her, his lips brushing her flesh. She moaned.

"Seems you need some help, too," she said, feeling his hard-on press against her.

He kissed the top of her head. "Always, where you're concerned."

She turned to him and removed her robe slowly, the

soft fabric sliding down her skin. Until Marco, she'd never felt comfortable being naked for the hell of it. Her parents, her father particularly, always preached modesty, and then growing up with big boobs had made her even more self-conscious. She loved her body but didn't find it necessary to parade her assets.

He gave her a look of sheer fascination, igniting a deep-seated desire in her for more. With Marco, nudity was natural. He took a couple of steps back as if to really admire her, and she found herself smiling.

"You're the most gorgeous woman I've ever seen."

Blood pounded in her veins, and a flush heated her face. She didn't believe it, what with the number of amazing models he must have dated. "You make me feel like that," she said honestly. If she gained nothing else from their time together—other than the deal they'd drawn—she would learn how good it felt to be cherished. Even if only sexually.

"I have something we'll try tonight," he said, then moved to his closet.

She touched the chair in front of a large rectangular, wood-framed mirror. His bedroom was so undeniable masculine. When he returned, he had removed his shirt and pants already, walking to her wearing just a pair of black boxer briefs that didn't conceal his erection.

He carried a bottle of lube in one hand, and in the other… She studied the short black device on his palm. "Touch it," he said, giving it to her.

She ran her finger along the ribbed texture, starting at the tip through the flanged angle. "What is this?"

And what would they do with it? She'd seen vibrators at bachelorette parties but never bought one herself.

"It's a butt plug."

She cleared her throat. Sweat broke on her forehead, and she clenched her thighs. So far he'd shown her a colorful world of pleasure and unknown sensations. A side of her wanted more, but what if—

"I can almost hear you thinking," he said, yanking her from her worries.

"Sorry. I... I've never done this before." She clutched the silicone device, warming it.

"Do you trust me to pop your ass cherry?" He lifted her chin until his gaze locked on hers. "This will only work if you do."

She nodded. "What's the plan?" She gave him the plug, and he put it aside, ushering her to the bed. He eased her down on the mattress, as if she were precious cargo. She propped herself on her elbows, unable to stay still.

He joined her in bed, still in his underwear, then covered her with his body and captured her lips with his in a languid, slow kiss. By the time their mouths disengaged, she struggled to breath, her heartbeat drumming in her ears.

"I'm not screwing your ass today. I'm just going to play with your hole, stretch it so when I fuck it... I'll make sure you enjoy it."

"If you say so. I trust you." Despite her insecurities, her clit throbbed in anticipation of all the sinful pleasures coming ahead.

He sucked her lower lip then released it with a pop. "Don't overthink it. If at any moment you want me to stop, just say so."

"Do we need a safe word?" She recalled a scene in a sexy movie where the male lead told his partner to use a word to halt things completely if needed.

He flashed her a boyish grin, so uncharacteristic of him. "I'm simple. If you say no, or stop, I'll stop."

She relaxed her shoulders and dropped to the mattress. "That's easy."

He lowered himself onto her, kissing her breasts, his

tongue lazily lapping one of the tips. She arched toward him, wanting to feel him on her even more. Whenever he kissed her, she always anticipated the next caress, the next touch, the next orgasm. She wrapped her legs around his ass in a silent plea.

He sucked her other breast, nibbling the tender area. She moaned and thrust her hips forward, experiencing a familiar buildup firing in her belly.

"You're ready for me, aren't you?"

"Yes."

He planted pecks on her stomach. "Good things come to those who wait."

"If you keep at it, I'll come even without waiting."

When he nudged her thighs apart and lowered his head in between them, she let out a whimpery sound she almost didn't recognize. He licked her, his tongue stroking her most intimate flesh, causing another coat of her own female lubrication. She loved how he ate her, with passion and reckless abandon.

She linked her legs around his shoulders, excited at the prospect of him diving into her wetness, losing himself inside her pussy. What she didn't count on was…he kept exploring her, his tongue tracing south of where he usually pleasured her. She gasped. Was he—

"Relax," he said. "I want to taste all of you Lily."

All? She relaxed her limbs, trusting he knew what he was doing. He licked the area near her hole, the tip of his tongue trailing a sinful path. Her instinct drove her to clench her thighs, but he patiently opened them and continued at it, upping the game by inserting two fingers into her pussy.

She moved her hips. He was kissing her asshole, licking her thigh, thrusting his fingers into her in a forward and reverse fashion. A tingle spread from her core to all areas of her body, turning into an extreme shiver. When he flicked her clit in addition to all the magic he worked on her, she called his name, her body shaking from top to bottom, sweat glistening her arms and chest.

A cold draft tickled her when he slowly rose from between her legs. That's the effect he had on her—he brought so much heat, but he also took it away. "I love to watch you come," he said.

She fanned over her flushed cheeks. "You kind of make it impossible for me not to."

"Good, but the fun is not over. Get on your hands and knees."

She gathered whatever strength she had and followed his command, turning onto her belly then lifting her ass in the air. She splayed her hands on the mattress like she was about to do push-ups, because she probably needed that kind of endurance. Gosh. She should work out more.

"What's on your mind?" he asked, and for a while he left the bed. She imagined he grabbed the lube and the butt plug.

"I was thinking I need to work out more often."

"You're gorgeous."

"So are you, but I bet that eight pack of yours doesn't happen overnight."

He chuckled. "Nothing in life happens overnight, my dear Lily... Actually, I'm wrong. You happened to me overnight, and I'm not sure I'll ever get over you."

His words cut a knife through her soul. She dared to glance at him over her shoulder, desperate to know if his voice had turned serious at the end or if she'd imagined things. When her gaze collided with his, moisture evaporated from her throat. Flecks of silver gleamed in his dark irises, giving him a mix of intensity and excitement. He watched her in silence, without wavering, as if he'd meant what he'd said. *I'm not sure I'll ever get over you.* What did his confession mean to him—to them?

Afraid she'd let him see right through her, she jerked her head back in place, away from him, but not from the madness flooding her.

Without saying anything, he propped her legs apart and touched her intimately. She didn't need this to confirm she was already soaking wet for him. Ready. Willing. She rocked her hips into his hands, hoping he'd get the hint and screw her until her world made sense again. Until his words had less meaning to her. Until she no longer entertained thoughts of admitting that she, too, would never get over him.

"Lily." He called her like a curse.

He drove his fingers into her hair, tugging it toward him. Her scalp sizzled, sending little charges through her. At the same time, he thrust his cock into her pussy, her walls stretching to accommodate him. He pulled her hair a little more, sending fiery sensations down her spine. Her skin goose bumped. She'd never been so primitively claimed in her life.

He released her hair and moved his cock out, then slowly in, making her squirm for more. Then she heard him picking up the lube. She heard him pop open the tube, then the sound of Marco rubbing it on his palm. As he thrust deep inside her pussy, she felt his finger, coated, slide between her ass cheeks. At first, her involuntary reaction was to expel him from there. She stiffened her back, unsure about what to do.

"It's new for you. If you trust me, we can have a lot of fun," he said from behind. "If not, it's okay."

His compromise rang in her ears. The fact he would be totally fine with her not trying anal sex, not seeing it through, caused her to let out a long exhale and say, "Keep going."

Why not judge for herself if she liked it or not? After all, her clit was throbbing, anticipating him touching her there, making her hotter than she'd ever been before. And she raised her ass, felt his finger push inside her, felt it close to the thin membrane separating his cock as he drove it inside her.

Her clit wanted to explode, the sensations firing through her, bringing her close, oh so fucking close to her orgasm. He withdrew his dick, then thrust into her again, deeper, harder. She threw her head back, reveling in how amazingly good it was to have him fully inside her, and not knowing where she ended and he began. While deep inside her, his balls at the base of her sex, he withdrew his finger from her butt, and she was about to ask why, when an instant later, she felt something bigger, longer, poke at her entrance. The plug.

No doubt to distract her, he drilled her pussy hard, delivering each thrust hotter than the last. She whimpered, pleasure coiling in the pit of her stomach. He inserted the plug all the way inside her and moved it in and out of her, mimicking the actions he did to her snatch, but with far less intensity. With his free hand, he made round circles on her ass, kneading her fleshy butt, palming her skin until it warmed under his sensual touch.

All of it was too much for her to keep track. She felt lightheaded, as the sensation of him ramming her both holes drove her insane…and she loved it. Every time he removed and thrust the plug from her ass, her nerve endings sizzled, that friction sending thrills down her spine. Damn, he'd been right.

"Marco," she called, knowing full well she was on the edge of climaxing.

He didn't relent, increasing the intensity of his cock fucking her while he plunged the plug into her faster, deeper, harder. She grasped the sheet, her fingers biting into the fabric as she balled her fists. So. Close.

He thrust into her pussy, her walls clinging to him, her inner muscles clenching around his hot rod. "Come for me, Lily. Show me how much you like being fucked in both holes by me. By only me," he said, then quickened the screwing of her ass, too, without mercy.

"Yes. Only you," she gasped, loving the sound of him slapping his body against her skin over and over again. Her clit pulsated, the achingly exquisite sensations increasing in intensity, sending an incredible surge of pleasure throughout her body until everything shattered, dizzying her, blinding her until she collapsed onto the bed barely able to breathe.

She felt him withdraw the plug, emptying her as he plunged into her pussy, stroking deep, fast, hard until he cried her name, jettisoning his release into her. Though about to pass out from the sheer magnitude of the aftershocks of her orgasm, she couldn't stop wanting to hold on to the moment, because having his cock buried deep inside her was amazing.

. . .

Marco steered his Ferrari through the wrought iron gates and into his grandmother's beautifully landscaped grounds. During the drive to Bellagio, one of the towns bordering Lake Como, memories from the previous night flashed in his mind. He kept his eye on the road and used small talking to dispel from his own senseless craving. Lily had been so hot for him, so willing.

"This is where your grandma lives?" Lily asked, looking everywhere, unable to hide the wonder in her voice. "It's beautiful."

The waterfront villa nestled in the mountains was breathtaking. "Yes," he said, contemplating the neoclassic mansion once he parked in front of it. That place had a historic value and been in his family for generations. It certainly would never be the same after Nonna passed.

A band squeezed around his chest for a while. A valet attendant walked up and kindly offered to park the car. The valet opened the door for Lily, and soon they both slid out and stepped toward the opulent entrance.

"I haven't been back in six years," he said, because he didn't want her to think he vacationed here often. What if she mistakenly lied about always wanting to accompany him in a trip, but couldn't because of her schedule? Everyone would know something was off.

"Why not? It's not like you have to save money for a trip. And you have an apartment in Rome."

"I come to Italy often. I've seen my grandmother a couple of times in Rome. I haven't been to the villa in six years, though."

"Why not?"

Because the older his grandmother got, the more endearingly overbearing she became. She often asked him a lot of questions about his dating life, his broken engagement, and once had brought the granddaughter of a friend to meet him, which embarrassed him. He could find his own woman—when he was ready to play that settle-down card. Nonna meant well, but it also meant every time he saw her he had to tread carefully around subjects he'd rather forget. "My grandmother is a lovely lady. She's one of the best parts of my childhood."

"Nice sentiment, but you still haven't answered my question."

He stroked her cheek. "Not everything is simple, Lily."

"It can be."

He curled his lips, entertaining a quick comeback, then settled for a smirk. Lily was uncomplicated and positive, untainted and hopeful. Were they really so different? He liked to think he was positive, in a pragmatic way. A realist. And every time he'd been naively hopeful, life had shown him what a fool he'd been. Yes, they were different. He clung to his contracts and structure as much as she clung to her dreams and faith.

"Whoa," she said, yanking him from his musing. "Unless

people sacrifice virgins inside, or the mansion is haunted, I can't fathom anyone choosing not to visit this place."

He looked at the imposing entrance. Purple saffron flowers outlined the stone path to the door. Before he knocked, his grandmother's longtime concierge, Marie, opened the door.

"Well, look at who the cat dragged in," she said, with her thick French accent. More than an employee, she had become his nonna's right hand and an honorary family member. The middle-aged brunette gave him a hug then patted his back. "Let me look at you, Marco Giordano. Every time I see you, I wish I were ten years younger."

"Why mess with Mother Nature's great work?" he asked. "This is my fiancée, Patricia."

"Fiancée!" Her hand flew to her chest. "Seriously? How nice. Debora will be overjoyed when she finds out."

"Hi," Lily said. "Nice to meet you."

Marie glanced at the hand Lily offered, but enveloped her in a hug. "Great to meet you."

Lily blushed, maybe overwhelmed with Marie's friendliness, but nevertheless she smiled. "Thanks," she said, regarding the two staircases on either side of the grand lobby. "This place is amazing."

"You haven't seen anything yet. Marco, when you said you were bringing company, I picked one of the rooms on the east side for you. Now I see she's family, I say we move you to your old room. Maybe your fiancée will appreciate your former stomping ground."

Irritation skated up his spine. "No," he said quickly. "I want one of the suites in the east wing." He had specifically requested one of them in his email. As far as he was concerned, they could burn his childhood room. He didn't want to set foot inside it, let alone share it with Lily.

Beside him, Lily stiffened, then flashed Marie a small

smile. "I'm sure any one of them will be perfect for us."

Maybe this had been a bad idea. While Marie talked Lily's ear off as they climbed up the curvy flight of stairs, he pretended to listen, but his mind raced. The idea of pretending to be happy, with his emotional life figured out, had seemed easy and simple. But now, with Lily here, he questioned his decision. This brought her too close to everything he wanted to forget, to erase permanently. Still, he wanted to give his grandmother a poignant, immaterial parting gift by faking his happiness.

He might have avoided seeing her, but they still called and talked regularly, because he meant what he said to Lily—his grandmother was one of the best parts of his childhood.

Now, however, every time they spoke, the silence after she asked him how he was had grown longer, and her sigh deeper. He'd wondered if Nonna knew what happened that night.

The night his mother died.

Chapter Eight

Lily slipped into the deep fuchsia cocktail dress. Because of the decadent color, the outfit didn't have any embellishments other than the soft, high-quality fabric. In fact, it was even conservative, with knee-length hem and a modest cut above her chest. She preferred it that way.

She applied makeup, choosing some dark shadow to enhance her eyes and a nude-colored lipstick. Her hair was up in a topknot. Where the hell was Marco? After they'd checked into their room, he did some business stuff while she surfed online. He'd been occupied with work, and she unpacked for the six days they were to stay, busying herself for most of the afternoon. An hour ago, he'd told her he needed to talk to his grandmother quickly, to tell her the news of the engagement himself.

Lily imagined he wanted privacy to catch up with his grandma before introducing her, and she respected that. She skimmed their enormous room, figuring not even honeymooners ever got such nice accommodations. The immense bed was raised, pinned by four posters, and adorned with sheer drapes that floated in the light breeze. They hadn't had time to make love, but she yearned for him to take her in that giant bed. Take her in the dirtiest way... Images of him thrusting into her ass populated her mind, and little thrills of anticipation tingled her insides, hardening her breasts.

She cleared her throat, yanking herself from a fantasy she was sure he'd turn into reality.

From the minute they'd arrived in Bellagio, she'd noticed the tension in the taut muscles stretching his shirt. He had to have a good reason to avoid seeing his grandmother all those years—if he didn't care for her, why come up with a fake engagement to give her something to smile about? Her stomach knotted. None of this was her business. Yet...

She slipped her feet into the nude Louboutin shoes and straightened her shoulders. Asking him to give her anything other than what he'd promised—hot sex—was dangerous. Determined to stop those furtive thoughts, she left the room. Surely, he'd meet her later.

Other than Marie, she hadn't met any of his family members or his grandmother yet. Anxiety cooled her skin with every step she took down the stairs. Once again, she found herself admiring those huge paintings, with pictures of what she imagined were former generations. The house had luxury, but an old-world quaintness also had its stamp on the furniture and accents. She stepped onto the distressed wood flooring at last, and this time quite a few people occupied the opulent living room, which was enormous, with double doors that opened to a terrace overlooking Lake Como.

"Miss?"

An impeccably uniformed waiter offered her some champagne. She picked a glass from the tray, thanking him quietly, then took the flute to her mouth and drank the entire contents in one gulp. By the time she set it on a nearby table, her limbs had loosened, and a delicious bubbly sensation overpowered her head, leaving her dizzy and relaxed. If everything else failed, drinking would be the best way to get through the next few days of pretending to be someone she was not.

A tall, red-haired woman in her forties walked up to her. She spoke Italian.

"I'm sorry, I don't speak Italian," Lily replied in English.

The woman smiled. "I said your dress is pretty. Who made it?"

She should have spent more time fumbling over the tag. "I'm not sure, to be honest. It's a spur of the moment purchase I made when I was in Bloomingdale's last week."

"I quite understand. I'm Arietta," she said, pronouncing her name with a sexy musicality Lily envied.

"Pretty name. I'm Lily, nice to meet you."

Arietta lifted her champagne flute. "Pleasure. I'm sorry for prying, but I haven't seen you in any of Nonna's previous parties. I would certainly have remembered."

"Yes. I haven't been in any of her parties. Haven't met her yet, actually. My fiancé brought me here."

Arietta's eyes gleamed, and she leaned closer, visibly interested. "How adorable. And who would that be?"

"Marco."

Arietta's expression froze for a moment, as if she was legit shocked about the news. Quickly, she blinked and recovered. "I didn't even know he was engaged."

"It happened quickly, but when you know, you know." That's what people said, anyway. The only thing Lily knew, or hoped, was that Marco wouldn't shun her for introducing herself before he'd had the chance to. Relax, her inner voice whispered. They had a fake story in place for a reason…for opportunities like this. Besides, she was being handsomely rewarded to be his fake fiancée. Which meant she should act like one at all times.

"What I know is, I can't wait to learn more about you, Lily," the lady said, bringing her arm to her.

Oh, shit. She'd given Arietta her real name! "Actually, my name is Patricia. I'm sorry. Lily is my middle name, and I use it sometimes as a pseudonym. I go by Patricia with my friends and family."

"Patricia Lily. What a cute combination."

"Actually, just Patricia please. Let's forget about Lily," she said, forcing a smile. She was so screwed. If Marco found out, he'd be less than thrilled. Apprehension pressed hard in her gut, and bile rose at the back of her throat. Crap. Crap.

"Sure. Well, you said you have a pseudonym. Are you an artist?"

Lily clasped her hands together, eager to ease the cold sweat breaking out on her palms. She sooo sucked at lying. "Unknown artist. I work with numbers...investments... In my free time I love to sculpt. I haven't found someone to represent me. It's more like a hobby," she added, unsure if she should shut up or keep going at this point. She had taken sculpting classes before she had to give them up due to the high cost. Those classes had been more of a stress relief when her father began to get sick.

"You don't say. That's terrific," Arietta said, tucking her arm into Lily's as if they were old friends strolling down memory lane. "Come with me. I'll introduce you around. You're such a treasure, I wouldn't dare keep you to myself."

"I—I should go find Marco." Lily was desperate to regain a shred of control. Was the woman being condescending, or did she genuinely like her and want to share the novelty of Marco's engagement with others?

"Nonsense. He'll find us. Have you met his father yet?"

Lily cleared her throat. Things were getting out of control fast. "Father? No, I haven't met his parents."

"Parents?" Arietta frowned. "You don't know?"

"What?" The third faux pas in five minutes? Cold sweat broke on her palms, and she used her free hand to smooth it on her dress. "What is it?"

Arietta's face softened. "His mother died when he was a child."

"Oh." Her cheeks burned. In reality, as a fiancée she should have known such basic information about his parents. If only the man weren't so freaking mysterious. "That's right. He...could have mentioned it before. How did it happen? I don't think I recall."

"She killed herself," Arietta said.

Lily's stomach sank to the floor. Her mouth fell open, and she touched her lips, but no sound came out. A wave of shock washed over, and slowly she managed to straighten her shoulders and recompose herself. She'd need a much stiffer drink than champagne to get through the rest of the evening.

• • •

Where in the hell was she? Marco strode through the crowd, but at each step a family member spotted him, slowing him down.

He didn't want to be a jerk, but the evening couldn't have been more complicated. He had gone to talk to his grandmother to deliver the news himself, before everyone noticing Lily's ring at the party.

Then, once he returned to the room, resolute to show off his tempting fake fiancée, she'd disappeared. When he went downstairs, he surveyed the interior, and a swish of pink caught his attention. Lily stood amongst a lively group made up of his gossip-extraordinaire cousin Arietta and a couple of other people he didn't recognize, other than... His heart skipped a beat. His father.

Why had they invited Calogero for a weeklong

celebration? His blood thrummed so hard in his veins, everyone's voices fell into the background for a moment. He wasn't sure if he was more pissed off at seeing Calogero after so many years, or finding him next to Lily, who seemed so comfortable.

"Patricia," he called to her.

She didn't answer, instead listening to what Arietta was telling her.

Of course. She wasn't used to being called that way. He walked around and slid behind her, nudging her elbow with the intimacy of a longtime lover. "*Tesoro*," he whispered.

She shivered and turned her head to him. "Marco."

"Marco. We've been talking about you," Arietta said, with her trademark half smile. "It's been so long." She kissed him on both cheeks, Italian style.

"Time has been good to you, Arietta," he said. He nodded to the other two men in the group, assuming they were friends of his younger cousins.

"Marco," his father finally said. One of the reasons Marco despised seeing his father, besides the reason he'd shoved into a vault long ago, was that the man looked like a sixty-something version of himself. This time, a more generous amount of gray blended with what was left of Calogero's brown hair. More creases gathered around his expressive dark eyes, a testimony of time. "We've been talking to this charming young woman who claims to be your fiancée."

"That's correct," he said, and held Lily from behind. His hands pressed her waist. Inwardly, he was grateful it gave his fidgety fingers something to do.

"Well, congratulations are in order," his father said, and Arietta nodded. "Have you seen your grandmother yet?"

"I just did. She can't wait to meet Patricia."

Lily smiled. "The feeling is mutual."

"Now, if you all excuse me, I need a few minutes alone

with my fiancée," he said.

Before anyone could respond, he took her hand in his and guided her to the terrace. The view was arresting, but there were still a few couples talking and gathering. He needed more privacy.

"What's going on?" she asked him.

He squeezed her hand and picked up the pace, leading her down the stairs to a tree-filled garden. When he'd been little, he played with his cousins in the yard, running and laughing, hiding and seeking. The few happy memories he had of his childhood popped into his mind, but he shook his head. He needed to think clearly, not to reminisce.

He guided her through the bushes until the buzz and music from the party decreased. The full moon illuminated Lily enough for him to see the outline of her face and lips. "What were you thinking?"

She threw her shoulders back, hands perched at her waist. "Excuse me?" The attitude in her voice annoyed him.

He gritted his teeth. "I asked you to wait for me."

"I'm sorry, but you were taking forever, and the party had already started an hour before I joined," she said. "I imagined you were busy with your grandmother. You told me you'd say hello to her, and when I left our room, you'd been gone for an hour. I came here to act as your fiancée, not to be treated like a Christmas ornament you only look at when you have to use it."

"Maybe I should have hired an actress instead, or someone who would follow my direction," he said. He paced in a small circle, crunching dry leaves under his heel.

"Sure, she would, as long as you didn't forget to tell her some critical information. Such as the fact your mother is deceased. That would have come in handy tonight."

He came to a halt, a chill snaking down his spine. "What?" The subject of his mother, his grandmother's daughter, was always delicate, and his family skirted around it, avoiding it as much as possible. He appreciated the silence as an adult, even if as a child he wished he'd had someone explain to him what was happening.

She angled closer to him, her expression softening. "How do you expect me to play my role if you won't let me in?"

"We talked about—"

"We talked about me, and our fake alternative world, but we never talked about you. I saw how you acted around your father. I'm not asking you to tell me anything I can use against you, but I need some pointers."

Who was she kidding? She could use anything against him if she needed. "That's why we have a confidential agreement."

"Exactly. You don't trust me," she said, her voice breaking. An emotion he didn't understand flickered in her huge green eyes, making him feel smaller than a grain of dirt. "I should go home. This doesn't feel real to me, even as fake as it is. You don't need me—you have your huge ego and secrets to keep you company."

She turned to go, but he clasped her elbow and pulled her to him. She lifted her chin, questioning his actions. Damn it, so did he. His gut tightened at the idea of her walking out of his life, of her denying him, of her leaving him. He'd dealt with his mother leaving him because of her illness, then Angelica because of the darkness in his heart. He swallowed. He wasn't done with Lily Jenkins.

"I need you," he said, before he dipped his head and crushed her mouth with his. She fought him for a moment, biting his lips, but soon, she fought him in a completely different way, adding so much passion to the kiss he almost fell backward. "Lily, I need you now," he said gruffly, terrified of how much he meant it.

Chapter Nine

Desire hit Lily like a violent blow. She wanted to scream at Marco, to make him understand her frustration, but the urgency in his voice melted away any resistance. She'd chastise herself later. Now, she needed to give in to the unbearable tension creeping under her skin.

"Marco... I need you, too," she said, unafraid to admit it out loud.

He pulled up her dress, and soon the coolness of the night whispered against her bare butt. "No panties. You'll destroy me one day, Lily Jenkins, and I'll let you."

His words rang in her ears and caused a silly amount of empowerment to bubble in her body. He turned her away from him, and she planted her hands on the trunk of a thick tree. A couple of sounds caught her attention—squirrels moving, him unbuckling his belt. When she touched the rough texture of the tree, she felt fresh sap under her palm.

Marco kissed her neck, and the image of that enormous bed in the suite they shared filled her mind. How nice would it be to screw in that sinful bed?

He nibbled her ear, and a shower of prickles washed over her, her nipples rock hard. "Lily," he rasped, and she wasn't sure if it was a plea or a demand. "Lily," he repeated in that rich, cultured voice that made her toes curl.

He nudged her thighs apart, and thrust his cock inside her, deep and hard. In any other circumstances, she'd complain about the lack of foreplay, but not this time. They both needed to fuck to clear their heads. Fucking had become both the problem and solution.

She rocked her hips into him, wanting to take him as deep into her as possible. He sank his teeth in the curve of her neck, and she moaned, the ripples of awareness drifting down her body. "So good."

"You're soaked. You were waiting for this, weren't you? For me to lose my mind and straight up fuck you in the middle of a party."

His words were an invisible force, pushing her to the edge. She fought to breathe, her breasts rising and falling. Could she fight his accusation? Sure, maybe she hadn't planned the seduction, but he brought out a naughty side of her that simply didn't care about anything else.

He retreated, only to ram harder into her, sending a delicious quiver to her entire being. A growl escaped his lips, telling her that he, too, was about to lose control. "Yes. You not wearing any underwear like a bad girl."

She moaned again.

He cupped her breasts, his fingers warming her painfully taut nipples through the fabric. She squirmed into him, on a sexual high.

"Tell me, baby, tell me all about how I make you feel, how bad you want me to fuck you hard and make you come."

Her clit tugged, pulsed, coiled with exquisite tension, the pressure building, building "I—I'm so close I can barely think." She just wanted him to keep fucking her until she reached the climax she craved, needed. Instead, he withdrew his cock from her, and she gasped. Her body shuddered, a chilly sensation enveloping her like she'd just entered some Alaskan igloo in her birthday suit.

"What's wrong?"

"Talk to me," he demanded behind her. "I want you to tell me what you want, Lily."

Talk to him? The argument started because *he* wouldn't talk to her, and now he was the one begging her for words? Dirty words. He squeezed her breasts. Shit. She needed to say something to resume her glorious trip to Poundtown.

He pulled her hair a little, an act so primal she couldn't stop her reaction, her response to him overwhelming, demanding more.

"I like when you screw me, hard and fast," she said, proud at the edge in her voice. "Your cock fills me perfectly... It's so thick and delicious."

The touch of his hands on her tits loosened, and soon he slid his fingers down her waist, clutching her sides. "Go on."

"I love that when we fuck, I feel like I belong to you. It's not dirty, but it's true. When you're inside me, I feel... safe. Cherished." *Like nothing can rip us apart.* The thought stabbed at her, and her heart thrummed wildly. *Please, don't care for him more than what was agreed. Don't care for him at all.* Her silent plea to her common sense was moot. A part of her already cared for him—immensely.

He positioned her so that she leaned onto the tree more, her ass in the air. She had half expected he'd leave her after her heartfelt admission, but he surprised her by driving himself into her again. "Like this?" he asked, his voice steady.

Her pulse raced at the base of her throat. "Yes. Yes, babe."

She turned her head to see him, and even with a sideway glance she spotted how intense, how dangerous he looked as he drove into her.

He pounded her, and her moans filled the space, lost into the mystery of the night, until finally her orgasm spasmed through her, overpowering her senses and dissipating all the tension from earlier.

Marco had the gift of making her forget everything around her, and maybe she had a similar effect on him—if the way he choked out her name as his cock shuddered with his own release was anything to go by.

He kissed her shoulder. "We should probably freshen up separately," he said, breaking the silence. "There's a bathroom nearby, next to the pool area."

She pulled down her dress. Some of his cum dropped down her thighs, and she closed her legs to keep it from sliding farther down. "Freshen up? We need to talk."

He stuffed his cock into his pants and zipped up. "We'll talk later."

She smoothed her hands over her dress, hoping it hadn't crumpled too much. "Later is now. Do you know I had to lie to your cousin about being an amateur sculptor?"

"What?"

"Yup. It's a long story, but my point is, why didn't you tell me about your mom? She committed suicide. That's a big deal."

He shoved a hand inside his pocket, then immediately removed it and rubbed the back of his neck. She didn't need to be a body language expert to know how difficult talking about his mother seemed for him.

She took one step in his direction, unsure of what to say but unwilling to drop the subject. If she'd ever have a chance to know him a bit better, this was it. "Tell me, Marco."

"My mother was mentally ill. Her schizophrenia came out after she had me. Until then, it had been latent, but some doctors say it takes something more difficult to bring out the first episode. Well, when I was born, I came early, and back then medicine wasn't as advanced as it is today. A few weeks early meant a lot more concerns. Anyway, she began to act strangely. They thought it could be baby blues at first. But my being born triggered it, and I don't think my father has ever gotten over that."

A surge of anger hit her, and she curled her fingers into a ball, wishing she could punch his father. She'd never imagined herself striking anyone, but now she seriously considered it. "That's ridiculous. You were a baby."

"As I grew older, she got worse. At first, they tried to downplay it, and hired the best doctors they could afford—always making sure she was on some treatment so she'd still be presentable at parties and social functions. She couldn't take the pressure." He said the last sentence with sadness.

"I'm so sorry. It must've been hard to see all that. Didn't your father help her?"

"They tried a couple of clinics. Sometimes she was gone for weeks at a time. The treatment back then wasn't as holistic and patient-centric as it is nowadays," he said.

She remembered an article she read about how much mental hospitals and wellness clinics had evolved through the decades. Her heart broke for his mother, assuming she never got the understanding she needed. "Didn't it help when she returned from the clinics?"

He sighed, looking into the darkness. "For a while, but then she'd revert back. Some nights Nico and I couldn't sleep with all the shouting between our parents."

She touched his shoulder but felt his muscles cord beneath her palm. He continued to look away. "That's awful," she said, knowing that, while she'd grown up without a lot of money, she'd never questioned her parents love for each other, or her.

She didn't go around him to face him directly, but didn't step back, either, sending him a comforting glance and still holding his taut shoulder.

"I don't want you to feel sorry for me. That's why I didn't tell you about my mother," he said, shrugging her hand away and facing her directly, making her stare at him whether she wanted to or not. "I didn't want to see this look in your eyes, like you wish you could take it all away."

"I don't feel sorry for you. I feel sorry for that child. The six-year-old," she said, and wondered how much of the six-year-old still inhabited the body and soul of the man standing in front of her.

"Fair enough. Well, I highly doubt this subject will come up again this week, but now you know."

She fought the need to give him a hug, knowing deep down he'd see it as a sign of sorrow. The tips of her fingers tingled to touch him, so she settled for brushing them on his hand. "Thanks for telling me. Was that why your ex-fiancée left you?"

"No," he said, jerking away and closing the subject. "Ready to freshen up then go?"

She wasn't. She wanted to ask more, to deep-dive into his soul, but she had to be content with the information he'd given her. His past, present, and future mattered to her, which rattled her so much that she knew she wasn't ready to hear his full disclosure yet, for fear it would mean the end of their agreement far sooner than she wanted.

• • •

"Nonna," Marco said, walking up to his grandmother.

He'd talked to her earlier, because he had wanted to break the news of his engagement firsthand. Now she sat at a table with a few lifelong friends, all the ladies wearing nice cocktail dresses. "This is Patricia," he said, still finding it difficult not to call her Lily. Patricia didn't suit her—it was too stuffy, too proper.

His lovely grandmother, still a big fan of chunky pearl necklaces and dark dramatic gowns, smiled at Lily. "So nice to meet you," she said with a strong Italian accent. "I prayed for the day my grandson would meet his match."

"So it's all your fault," Lily said, shaking her hand.

The two women shared a laugh, and lightness washed over his being. Despite the mishap earlier, he had to admit he'd made the right choice. Lily might not notice, but as she spoke to Nonna, people around them watched her.

Arietta kept an eye on her, from two tables away. He shook his head. His cousin would no doubt tell his brother the news upon his arrival later. He'd toyed with the idea of telling Nico himself; his jaw would drop to the floor.

"You're stunning, my dear," his nonna said. "And you managed to straighten out my grandson, so I'll forgive that you aren't Italian."

Lily chuckled, taking it stride. "Thank you. You know, my not speaking Italian is an advantage. If I knew what he says in Italian when he's angry, maybe we wouldn't be here today. Together."

Nonna's lips broke into another smile, filling his heart with pride. "I like you already, Patricia."

Lily saw an empty chair next to her and sat down. "The feeling is mutual. Marco told me a lot about you."

Nonna waved her off, leaning closer. "Don't believe him, they're all lies."

Lily winked at her. "That's what I thought."

He watched them chat, taken aback for a moment. Lily would be the last of his dates his grandma would ever meet. Nonna had never liked Angelica much, especially after the end of their relationship. He'd kept from introducing random affairs to her as a sign of respect, and also for self-preservation. Yet, a strange emotion delved into his chest, as if him introducing Lily to Nonna represented some closure. Lily was doing a pretty damn good job, too.

"*Primo*," said a voice he recognized behind him.

"Arietta," he called, turning around to greet her.

"Your fiancée is quite something," Arietta said. "She's drop-dead gorgeous, smart, and even seems to have fallen on Nonna's good side." If the words complimented, Arietta's tone did not. It sounded more accusatory than kind.

"She's the total package," he said, choosing to ignore the snarkiness in Arietta's voice. Arietta had been Angelica's best friend growing up, and never approved of them breaking up. Marco never discovered what Angelica told friends and family, but somehow Arietta seemed to think he'd been the jerk and done something unforgivable. *Maybe she knows the truth. That's why she doesn't want to see me happy.*

"Yes. By the way, you do know I donate to a local artistic organization, right?" she said, switching to a lighter tone.

In the past decade, he'd stayed away from his drama-prone cousin as much as he could manage. Nothing more than a quick chat here and there. "No, I didn't."

"Well, your fiancée has been generous enough to trust me with her secret."

He frowned. "Secret?" Shit. Lily was just too trusting if she'd told Arietta anything.

A glint sparked in Arietta's big eyes. "Yes. Her hidden talent."

What the hell? Afraid to let out more than needed, Marco nodded as if he knew what the hell she was talking about.

"I was wondering if she'd mind coming over tomorrow for a quick visit. We have some children from a local school visiting the studio and I'm sure they'd love to meet an international artist. That would mean the world to them."

"I think we're fully booked."

"I understand, but if she spared thirty minutes from

her day, I'd be so grateful. If not, maybe we can ask her new best friend to sway her," she said, her head pointing in the direction of their grandmother.

A flare of irritation ignited through him. Damn Arietta. "Fine. Thirty minutes and that's it." Whatever plan Arietta had to embarrass his fiancée, he'd be one step ahead of her.

A smile of triumph formed on Arietta's face. "Thanks, Marco, for being so accommodating."

He waited patiently until the end of the evening, after dinner and dessert, when he and Lily were headed back to their suite, to ask her, "What did you say is your hidden talent?"

"Sculpting."

"Sculpting?"

"Yes. It's a long story, but I introduced myself as Lily at first, then I realized I made a mistake, so I said Lily was a pseudonym for my amateur artistic side."

Wrong name. Shit. No wonder Arietta walked around like she knew the secret numbers of a winning lottery ticket. His cousin suspected his fiancée was not who she said she was, and if Arietta mentioned that to Nico, all would be lost. Nothing could stop those two from tearing Lily's identity apart. While Nico would do it for the "greater good" of their company, he wouldn't boast about his findings to Nonna or anyone else. Even when they disagreed, he and his brother had each other's backs.

But the same couldn't be said about Arietta. She'd find pleasure in outing Marco's plan publicly. "No wonder Arietta was all over you. She suspects something's off."

"Oh, crap. You hate me, don't you?" She chewed on her lower lip.

Hate her? He wished. Hating her would make his life easier, hating her wouldn't cause his body to go into overdrive when she smiled at him or called his name. "No."

"Look, I'm sorry. I dropped the ball. Even though you prepared me so much, I'm not a natural liar—preacher's daughter, you know."

"It's okay. We'll figure it out. Arietta only wants you to meet some children who are visiting an art studio. It's not like you're expected to teach them about sculpting. Google some stuff about the craft and you can interact with the children for a while. Do you like children?"

"Yes, of course."

Of course she did—Lily had "wife material" written all over her. She'd probably make a good mom, too, one day. He frowned at his own random thought. Why did he care? "Good."

She switched her weight from one foot to the other. "Still, I feel bad for making it harder. If there's anything I can do to make life easier, please let me know," she said, winking at him at the end.

Now that proposal he could handle. That offer he could take. "I can think of something."

She inched closer, mischief gleaming in her eyes. "Really? What is it?"

"I want you to wash my hair."

"Come again?" she asked, inclining her head to the side as if she didn't hear him correctly.

"I was so aroused when you washed my hair when we first met. It was very erotic and made me want to take you on the spot," he said, his confession evoking sexy memories and provoking a stir in his insides.

"Well, then, get ready."

He smiled—knowing full well his hair wasn't the only thing about to get wet.

Chapter Ten

Lily lit the vanilla-scented candles then put the lighter back into a drawer. She'd snuck out of the room and asked Marie for candles and a lighter, and the sweet lady gave them to her quickly, no questions asked. She scanned the majestic bathroom, which looked like something straight from the pages of an upscale decorating magazine. Ever since she'd arrived that morning, she'd been dying to take a bath in the oversize marble tub. But she hadn't had the time, so she'd chosen the stand-in shower instead.

Now she had a much better reason to use it with Marco.

She withdrew travel-size shampoos from her toiletry bag. When he'd admitted how much he enjoyed the way she made him feel when she washed his hair, something warm and fuzzy had enveloped her. She'd expected him to be mad for the setback she'd caused regarding his cousin, but he surprised her by finding a way to work together in the end. Would he be like this in a real relationship?

Lily snorted. Yeah, like it mattered. She'd never know. He'd been clear from the start about his intentions. In fact, he'd paid her so there wouldn't be any lines crossed. Shaking her head, willing away any silly hope of their hot sex contract leading to something more, she took the luxurious shower gel from the cabinet. Several exquisite bottles occupied the three shelves, filled with all kinds of skin care and beauty products.

She turned on the tap, made sure the warm water filled the tub, and poured in a generous amount of gel. Quickly, bubbles formed, and a white foam took over the tub. Hmmm... He'd asked her to wash his hair. What was stopping her from joining him?

Not a thing.

Liquid heat pooled in her core. She peeled off her clothes and folded them on a chair. Then, she picked the bottles she'd need and placed them on a stool next to the tub. Giggling, she stepped inside and sank into the hot, scented bath, luxuriating in the water as it skimmed over her bare skin and covered her breasts. The foam kissed the tips of her nipples, making them pebble into taut points. "You can come inside," she called, already anticipating him coming in her.

The door swung open, and he greeted her with the most gorgeous, devilish smile on his face, his eyes darkening as soon as his gaze landed on her. "Well, well... This should be fun."

"I figured it'd be easier to wash your hair if I'm in here."

He removed his shirt and dropped it to the floor. "Of course."

He pulled down his pants and underwear in one swift movement and shoved them to the side. God, he was beautiful. She gave herself a few seconds to gape at him, appreciating how his muscles moved as he walked up to her. The ridges and planes of his body were like a map she wanted to explore again and again.

She didn't allow her gaze to slide past his six-pack, knowing full well she'd find a hard-on waiting for her. A delicious current went up her spine. How in the heck would she be able to do what he asked when she wanted to fuck him right now? She had to be strong and wait to give in to her arousal, which would only make the sex even better.

She scooted against the end of the tub. "I want you to sit between my legs, with your back against me."

"But then I'd be missing out on the view."

"I need to do a good job. Just follow my lead for once."

He let out a sigh of amusement, with the silent statement he doubted either of them would manage to keep their hands off each other for long.

When he dipped down in front of her, she wrapped her legs around his torso and lifted a bit so she'd be taller than him.

"If anyone opened a hair salon with this technique, they'd become a billionaire overnight," he said.

She chuckled and reached for the bottle on the chair. She opened the cap, added some water, and splashed some of it in his hair, wetting it until the ends curled under her touch. She heard a groan from him. They hadn't even started, and he was already out of sorts.

"Hair washing is one of my favorite things to do. I know it must be so uninteresting to a guy who takes out CEOs and the like," she said, wondering about the kind of women he dated. Did he prefer powerful business types who knew the score? Or long-legged top models? A Google search would give her the answer, but her stomach tightened with dread.

"You're the most interesting person I've ever met," he said.

Her heart flipped, and she almost wished she could excuse herself and go deal with her unleashed emotions in private. He hadn't asked her to move in with him, for crying out loud. He hadn't even offered her any clues that he'd like to take her on something as trivial as an actual date after their contract came to an end.

She swallowed. He'd complimented her on something other than her looks, or her sexual skills, and the part of her that yearned for acceptance was far too excited. More excited than she was by the way his back rubbed against her sensitive nipples, sending electrical charges into her clit, making it pulse. "Thanks. You're not bad for a money-hungry Italian billionaire. Because I meet those every day, you know."

For a time that stretched for longer than she counted, she massaged his scalp, her fingers working through his hair. His shoulders relaxed, and she felt rather than heard his sigh. He enjoyed this. "You weren't kidding me, huh. You like me to play with your hair."

"I'm sure if you find a shrink, she'll say I wasn't touched much as a child."

"Were you?"

"Not really. I got used to it, though."

"Did your brother suffer the same scrutiny you did growing up?" she asked. The little he told her always involved him being shunned, but nothing about Nico. She hadn't met Nico yet, so she couldn't appraise if the treatment he received from their father was as cold and distant as it was for Marco.

"No. He was born already, and our mother didn't have any problems when he was the only child. When she became pregnant with me, she had a complicated pregnancy and after my early arrival, she started to lose it."

"Did your brother ever tell you if he remembers any episodes, any events prior to you being born? Mental illness doesn't happen overnight."

She watched his back muscles tensed temporarily, and she squeezed him tighter for a moment, hoping her silent act of encouragement would keep him talking. "It doesn't. She was a brilliant woman, I hear. She married at eighteen and got pregnant soon after. She had a somewhat erratic behavior, but my father, being older, assumed it was an age thing. When I came along, she found herself with a toddler and a baby, and it was too much for her to handle."

She drifted her hand down to his shoulders for a moment and traced an invisible pattern on his flesh. "Didn't she have help?"

"Yes, but my father played dumb at first. He didn't want to admit she had problems until the situation spun out of control."

"It was probably hard for him to see her that way," she said, by no means justifying his actions. "When my father was diagnosed with cancer, my mom took it pretty hard. They were happily married, and she knew he wouldn't make it for a long time," she said.

"I'm sorry. Sounds like you were very close to him."

"I was. He was a straight shooter, but also protective of me," she said, finding it difficult to continue speaking without a strained voice.

Closing her eyes, she willed away the sadness lurking under the surface. Maybe her father wouldn't approve of her recent decisions, but he still would want her to live her life and not succumb to melancholy every time she remembered him. *Happy memories. Think about happy memories.* "Every birthday he gave me a bouquet of lilies. That was our thing. One night, I went out on a date and came home way before my curfew. I didn't say anything, but he could see in my eyes I'd been crying. I felt embarrassed. My mother was working until late that Saturday in the beauty shop." She grabbed a small decorative glass bowl and turned on the tap to pour some water and remove the shampoo from his hair. Then she added some minty conditioner and continued to massage his head.

"What happened?" he asked.

"The next day, I woke up and there was a vase filled with lilies on my nightstand. He must have left at night or early in the morning to buy those for me. It was his quiet way of cheering me up, saying he was there for me."

"No wonder you have a great head on your shoulders."

She could laugh at the irony—she'd agreed to screw him for a month for very wrong reasons. Since when did that make her remarkable in any way? She pursed her lips, deciding to keep the mood light. "Does this feel all right?" she asked, deepening the pressure on his scalp.

"Hmmm."

She took that as a yes. "Maybe after this crazy month is over, you can visit me at the shop once in a while. You know, to make sure your hair is being washed properly," she said, and a second later, bit her lower lip so hard, she swore she tasted blood. *Idiot, idiot.* She opened her mouth to take it all back, but only managed to let out a groan filled with regret. Shit.

"Thanks. I'll keep that in mind."

Sweat broke on her forehead, and it had nothing to do with the warm water or the proximity to his body. "Forget it; that was a bad idea." In her unadventurous and somewhat limited love life, she'd never really asked guys out or imposed relationship rules. She'd been happy to play along if the men were good guys who cared about her. And now, for some reason, the idea of parting from Marco upset her, made her frustrated and sad, and at the same time—

"No," she said out loud.

He turned around until he faced her, his hair still mussed from her hands. "What?"

"I'm sorry. I was thinking if I had DVRed *Game of Thrones*, and I realized I forgot to do it," she said, waving it off.

He flashed her a smile, but there was a flicker of regret in his eyes. She wondered what it meant, but he shook his head, maybe willing intrusive thoughts away. He cupped her cheeks, making her stare at him. "You're adorable, Lily

Jenkins."

"Are you being condescending?"

"No. I mean it. I don't think I can visit you at work, though, because one day I'll see you and you'll be with a boyfriend. A man who deserves you. A man who will bring you lilies."

Why can't you bring me lilies? The thought stabbed at her before she could shake it off. She hated herself for the strand of disappointment in her chest. "And you say that just like that?"

"I want to see you happy."

"What about you? What would make *you* happy?"

His jaw clenched, a silent warning he really didn't enjoy talking about the future—his or hers. "Happiness for me isn't the same it is for most people. I…haven't been given lilies, so I don't know where to start. I like to know what to expect from people. I like to be in control, even if I miss out on other things. That's how I operate."

She made an effort to keep a neutral expression so he wouldn't pick up on the nugget of frustration. "That sucks."

He lifted his hand and caressed her cheek. His touch was like a miraculous cream on a wound. "It does. That's why I'm focusing on what's bringing me joy right now…and that's you," he said hoarsely. A warm expression washed over his face, the heat of his gaze burning her flesh. "You're vibrant, real, honest."

Her breath caught in her throat, and she opened her mouth but hesitated. Why did he have this delicious quality of making her feel so unique? And why, even with all those compliments he gave her, did he still believe they couldn't have a future? A real one?

He pulled her to him, and she sat on him, her legs to his sides. "Come here. It's been far too long since I was last inside you."

Chapter Eleven

"Our engagement is fake, but the way you send me into overdrive is all too real," he said, meaning every damn word. He covered her lips with his, and she opened her mouth to him, granting full access. Delving his tongue inside her, he rejoiced.

Maybe he shouldn't have told her so much about his life, but she made it all too easy to open up and share. And now, to keep from thinking about the consequences of his own actions, he'd fuck her like he was born to do.

Tongues melded, he slid one hand down her back, caressing the area between her butt cheeks. She shifted on top of him, making it easier for him to knead her plump ass.

Ever since she began touching him, stroking his scalp with vigor, his cock had engorged. A rush of blood traveled south in his body, and every part of him was in complete awareness of her tits rubbing against his chest, her teeth grazing his lower lip.

She disengaged her mouth from his, panting. "Marco, I don't know if I can last long."

He kissed her nose. "That should be my line. You've been teasing me with your hands for a while. We need to get even."

She nibbled his jaw, sending currents of electricity through his body. "I'd like to see you try."

Marco tugged at her hair, bringing her face down so she had to stare at him. Challenge gleamed in her extraordinary green eyes. He maintained the gaze for a moment, without loosening his grip. She moaned, and her nipples rubbed against his chest, the tips hard and tight. Slowly, he dipped his head to close the gap between them, until his face was a breath from hers. She parted her lips in a silent plea for him to end the torture. Too bad he was enjoying the game, even if his cock throbbed painfully.

"Please…" she said, her voice above a whisper.

"What? What did you say?" he asked, tilting his head to the side, pretending he hadn't heard her.

She lifted her chin to end the distance between them, and he pulled her hair back a bit, pinning her to his complete advantage. She closed her eyes for a moment, and he imagined the sensations overwhelming her.

He loosened his grip on her hair until his hand traveled down her stomach, and soon he inserted two fingers into her wet pussy. She arched toward him, her eyes opening with a start, her breath coming out labored. Lily was like an exotic fruit, delicious and ripe for the taking.

With his other hand, he continued to massage her ass in circular movements, each time his fingers landing closer and closer to her puckered hole. He enjoyed touching her, playing with her, teasing her…making her his.

She pulled his head down, kissing him with fervor, her lips searching, her tongue stroking his without mercy. He added another finger to work her pussy, loving how wet and ready to be fucked she was…all for him. "Marco," she called, withdrawing her lips from his momentarily. "Keep doing this.

Touching me."

"In the front or the back?"

"Both, babe. Feels so good when you fuck me like that."

Encouraged, he intensified his thrusting and retreating out of her pussy. If they weren't surrounded by water, he'd hear the sound of his fingers slapping her each time they entered her snatch or backed away. Now, his arm made little waves around them, and soon water splashed out of the tub, but he didn't care. He continued the menacing rhythm, dead set on pleasuring her, and at the same time, slipping his index finger into her hole.

She yelped and gave a little jump, but didn't jerk away. She thrust her hips into his finger, moaning, her eyes half closed. "I want your cock buried inside me," she said in a voice so raw, so honest, he couldn't resist.

As much as he wanted to extend their foreplay, he couldn't. Marco removed his fingers from her pussy and replaced them with his cock, adjusting her position enough so she accommodated him. He should give her complete control this once, and let her set the rhythm, but he didn't resist. With one hand still squeezing her ass cheeks, he gripped the edge of the tub with the other and began pounding her.

"More," she whispered.

He moved his finger in her asshole, mimicking how his dick rammed her in and out. Soon, his own world began to collide, a powerful surge of pleasure igniting in his core and spreading all over him. He intensified his claim on her, fucking her deep, making her shake. Her sexy moans filled the air, her neck vein pulsating. Following her cue, he let go, climax drilling through him until a growl was the only sound he managed to produce.

She rested her head on the curve of his neck, still quivering. He pulled his cock out of her, and carefully removed the finger from her back entrance. Kissing the top of her head, he sighed. No matter how much either of them tried to dictate the rhythm of that screw, their desire had become a force of its own.

• • •

"More coffee?" Lily asked Marco, holding the container.

"No, thanks," he said, watching her pour some more black liquid into her mug and sit next to him. Damn it. If it'd been up to him, he'd have used the machine in his room and not come to the outdoor terrace to have breakfast with everyone. Thankfully, after a quick round of small talk, his uncles and aunts had left the area to prepare for the day's activities.

Besides a few distant cousins whose name he didn't recall right away, they were alone. Most people must have eaten earlier, his grandmother included. He chugged his remaining coffee, and this time the drink rolled thick and cold in his throat. Why was Lily being so nice to him after what he'd said the previous evening? She had proposed, subtly of course, that they still see each other after the end of the contract.

He'd heard that glimmer of hope in her voice. What if she wanted more from him, more than he could give? He'd been honest from the beginning. Maybe she wanted to renew the contract, which would be ludicrous. What else could she possibly want from him after he'd paid her debts and secured her salon?

His gut clenched. Money. She'd need money for advertising to promote her salon. After all, if she didn't do anything drastic to get more clients, she'd be in a dire situation soon. A monthly allowance, perhaps?

"Hey. What are you thinking about?" she asked, nudging his elbow.

"I'm thinking we should go sightseeing before my cousin

gets her claws into you," he said. What he really wanted to say was how he'd also thought about visiting her salon even after their affair ended. The idea seduced him, slowly, lethal like a poisonous snake carefully dancing her way out of a charmer's box.

"Sounds great. We can leave after I finish eating," she said, taking a bite of *fette biscotatte*, the hard bread smothered in Nutella. "This is delicious."

"It is," his brother said behind him, surprising them with his presence. "Nico Giordano," he said, gazing at Lily.

Lily covered her mouth for a moment, blushing, still eating the pastry, then she quickly swallowed it and said, "Oh. Nice to meet you. I'm Patricia."

"Patricia. Trust me, the pleasure is all mine." Nico pulled out a chair and sat. "Hey, brother. You never told me you'd bring your beautiful friend to Nonna's party."

"I like to throw a curveball once in a while," Marco said.

"A hell of a curveball," Nico said, scratching his five o'clock shadow. "Then Arietta calls me and says you're engaged. Imagine that. My confirmed bachelor of a brother, getting hitched."

His throat grew thicker in annoyance. Marco wished he could take his brother into a martial arts studio and solve their differences over there. "I wanted Nonna to be the first one to know."

"Is that why you didn't tell me?"

"Yes. Besides, you're not my mother. I love you, brother, but I don't need your permission," Marco said, his voice as firm as his conviction.

Nico hesitated for a moment, probably pondering if fighting Marco was worth it. He settled for a slow nod. "Understood. Well, congratulations to both of you." Nico smiled.

"Thanks," Lily said.

"How did you two meet?" Nico asked, darting his gaze from Marco to Lily. "I can't wait to know all about my future sister-in-law."

Marco curled his fingers into a ball. The less he told his brother, the better. He didn't need to be a rocket scientist to know Nico saw through their facade, or at the very least, questioned their relationship. Like Nico gave two shits about how they *actually* met. "At a bar," he said. "The rest is history."

Lily shifted in her seat. "How about you, Nico? Are you seeing anyone?"

"Not currently. You need to tell me the type of bars in New York you're going to where you're meeting such gorgeous women. Sorry, I didn't catch your last name, Patricia."

"Doors. Patricia Doors."

Nico frowned. "Interesting."

Marco pushed his chair and stood up, then swiftly pulled Lily's out to prompt her to rise as well. "We'll chat more later. I promised Patricia I'd show her Bellagio today."

Nico gave her a lingering glance, and Marco could almost see the wheels turning in his brother's brain. Nico pursed his lips, his neutral expression not fooling Marco for a nanosecond. "Sounds good. See you guys soon."

He guided her through the house, taking a shortcut to make it out as fast as possible. Once they were inside the car, he let out an exhale. His brother thought he had his back, and if for some reason he didn't believe their story, Nico wouldn't rest until he proved his case. Damn him.

"Do you think he bought it?" Lily asked, turning her head around as if to make sure they weren't being followed.

He chuckled. "This isn't a spy movie. Relax, Nico isn't behind us."

"Does your brother know about your contract shenanigans?"

"I don't discuss details of my intimacy with him, but he knows I prefer things clearly discussed upfront," he said. Nico wasn't exactly the domesticated kind, either. He'd even mentioned once he planned on getting a vasectomy because he didn't want to inflict pain on his children like his father had done to them.

"Why didn't you tell him about our fake engagement? You two seem close."

"Because this is more complicated. If I tell him the truth, he'll know about the garage. I'll tell him after everything is said and done."

"He'll think you lost it over my heavenly pussy," she said with amusement.

Marco should have said something and joined the fun, but a growing concern kept him from joking about what had become an almost palpable fear. His obsession over Lily and all her body parts was no laughing matter.

• • •

They'd spent the morning visiting the historic downtown in the nearby town of Como. With Lily, Marco had looked at the basilicas as if seeing them for the first time. He'd appreciated walking with her along the curvy, winding roads, telling her about the town and the several others in the region. He almost wished they had more time to see more together. Oh, the cities he could show her, not only in Italy. He'd love to bring her to Athens. Sydney. London.

"Are you ready for this?" she asked when he parked in front of the art studio Arietta had suggested they visit. They could balk and leave, but that would only enhance Arietta's interest in their situation—which, in turn, would add fuel to his brother's curiosity. Best to deal with the problem up front.

"Yes. We go in, shake some hands, and you say how much

you love painting—"

"Sculpting." She cut him off, rolling her eyes.

"Yes. Of course."

"Can I confess something?"

"Indulge me."

She leaned closer, and he caught a whiff of her feminine scent. "I had the highest marks in my sculpting class."

"Great. So this shouldn't be so hard."

He slid out of the car, went around the vehicle, and opened the door for her. She wore a yellow dress that made her look impossibly carefree and young. He wished he could take her in the car, or behind an alley, to address his rising internal temperature. What if he continued to find it increasingly difficult to come to terms with the fact they'd say goodbye in two weeks? Could he let her go? Would he?

She grabbed his hand in hers, an intimate gesture that came naturally to them, and one he'd never really appreciated prior to meeting Lily. Walking hand in hand never seemed like a necessity, especially for an experienced man like himself. He felt her palm sweaty against his. She was nervous about putting on this sculpting act, but not once did she try to convince him to walk away.

They entered the studio, where a plethora of artwork was displayed on small stands. Remarkable canvases for sale hung on the walls, as well as framed photos of famous celebrities who had visited the place. She squeezed his hand, and in response, he made an invisible pattern on her palm with his thumb, hoping the continuous movements soothed her.

She gave him a sideways glance, a mischievous gleam in her eyes like they communicated in their own secret language. A tremor traveled through him.

"There you are!" Arietta called, jerking him out of his thoughts as she strolled up to him from the opposite side of the room. "Come here. The kids are dying to meet Patricia."

It was his turn to tighten his grasp on Lily's hand, bringing her closer.

They walked in tandem to the door and found a room where several kids talked vivaciously. When they entered, a few of them continued chatting, but most grew quiet and watched them, Lily especially. What the hell had Arietta promised them to make them so interested in her?

"*Ciao*," Lily said, letting go of his hand. "Thanks for the opportunity, Arietta," she said, giving his cousin a hug.

Arietta's face froze for a moment, but she quickly recovered and responded to the spontaneous embrace. A wave of pride threaded down his spine. Lily managed to disarm his overbearing cousin in a few seconds. Nice start.

"Thank you for coming, Patricia. They're thrilled to see you. I told them not to hold their breath because you're so busy, but they'd love if you showed them some of your skills. Maybe they'll learn something new from you." She winked at her.

"Or I'll learn something new from them." Lily said, studying the material displayed on the tiled counter next to a big sink. "You do water-based sculptures?"

"Yes. Natala here works at this studio and allows children to visit every month for special classes," she said, pointing at a young woman with lustrous, long hair.

"Great. Why don't you have a typical session with them, and I can supervise what they do in a case-by-case basis?"

"Good idea," Natala said, with a heavy accent. "We've been working on vases."

"Always a good start to do confined shapes," Lily said.

Natala translated the idea to the children, and a few of the boys kept their gaze on Lily.

"Let's do this," Lily said. He knew her well enough to sense a tremble in her voice. What sounded like excitement to others carried a pang of apprehension to him. Regardless, she soldiered on, and soon the children made a line to wet the clay and begin working and playing with it.

His throat thickened. He should walk around and interact with the students, but he only had eyes for Lily. His Lily. What kind of child would he have been if he had a mother like her? What kind of adult would he have turned into—perhaps one less tainted, less objective, more susceptible to society's idea of normal? A man who didn't hide behind contracts and the ink of a pen to keep his emotions in check. A braver man.

A little boy with curly blond hair walked up to him, his eyes twitching like he was about to cry. "Sir, can you help me?"

He kneeled to look the kid in the eye. "I'm not great at this stuff, but I can try."

"I wanted to make a vase for my mom."

"Then a vase we shall make," he said, and grabbed an apron hanging on the wall. For the next few minutes, they tried molding the clay into a bowl. The boy seemed more relaxed, smiling on occasion, talking about airplanes and dinosaurs. Marco could have given the little guy a prize and thanked him for taking his mind off Lily. At least, for the moment…

Chapter Twelve

"Look at you. You could pass for a pro," Arietta said, behind her.

Lily took a deep breath. She had watched a few YouTube tutorials to refresh her rusty memory, and doubted she'd have pulled it off if her audience had been more discerning. The little kids, though, enjoyed her visit, and her idea of observing and encouraging them instead of putting on a demonstration had paid off.

"They're children," she said. "It's more liberating to let them work freely than restricting them to one way of doing things."

"True," Arietta said. "Feel free to give them tips, though, to make their sculpting process more efficient. Even though you aren't getting paid yet in the United States, you must have some time-saving tips."

Lily squared her shoulders. No way would she pretend more than she knew and fall into Arietta's trap. "Art is art anywhere in the world, and it can't be rushed. Now, if you'll excuse me," Lily said, walking past the woman to check the stations. Phew.

For some reason, Marco's cousin wanted her to fail. She wanted her to admit she didn't know much and certainly couldn't add any to what these kids already knew. A few times she had to pull answers out of her ass, but she hoped plastering a smile on her face while she did it helped her convince them.

She didn't want to screw things up for Marco.

Instinctively, she turned her head in his direction. For the past half an hour, he had been assisting an adorable young boy, maybe six or seven. Her heart filled with bursting bubbles of joy. She hadn't seen him with kids yet, and had expected him to be the kind of guy who treated little ones as adults and miss out on the quirks of childhood.

She'd been wrong.

He hadn't found an excuse to get rid of the boy, or asked for someone else to facilitate. They'd been working hard together, and she wished she could speak Italian to understand what stories he told to make the boy laugh with gusto.

"How are we doing?" she asked, inching closer to them.

Giuseppe—that's what his name tag said—looked up at her. He spoke quickly, gesturing with his hands in a frantic attempt to tell her something.

"What is he saying?" she asked Marco while touching the boy's hair to acknowledge him.

Marco sighed. "He feels bad we've been trying to do a perfect vase for his mom, but the edges still came out rough," he said, pointing at their imperfect piece. Giuseppe spoke again, and Marco translated. "He wants her to be proud of him."

She kneeled down and lifted Giuseppe's chin up. "Can you please tell him I'm proud of him?" She looked into the boy's eyes but spoke to Marco.

Maybe Giuseppe sensed her approval, for a shy smile formed on his lips.

"Tell him sometimes when we start our process, we have an image in our minds of what the final piece will look like. We work toward that goal, then things change. They don't go as planned, and that's absolutely fine."

Marco translated her words in his dreamy voice.

"Tell him this bowl is unique because he made it and his mother will love him for it. If she doesn't, she can talk to me. I'll set her straight."

Giuseppe giggled, and even before Marco told him what she'd said, she knew he had understood her intent.

When she peered at Marco again, she noticed a strong emotion flashing in his cocoa eyes. Flecks of gold sparkled in his irises, like shooting stars in a dark sky. Her heart stopped in her chest, and she watched him, hypnotized, unable to speak and ignoring everyone around them.

The need to hug him, to kiss him, to claim him, ignited at her core and spread madly throughout her body. Her own words played in her mind like an old broken record. *We work toward that goal, then things change.*

Shit. The situation hadn't changed—they were still in Italy pretending to be committed to each other when the only thing drawing them together, besides scorching sexual chemistry, remained a calculated contract. No, the situation hadn't changed, but she had.

Oh, crap. I've fallen in love with Marco.

• • •

"You were great with the children. Arietta didn't suspect a thing," he said, as they entered their suite.

The day had been long, with him showing her the sights then the stop at the art studio. All she wanted was to throw herself in his arms, but they had one last activity—a mandatory one. His aunt had planned for everyone to go on a boat trip along Lake Como, with drinks and more fancy appetizers, she imagined.

"Thanks. What should I wear tonight? I'm assuming it's not a jeans-and-sneakers type of event, right?"

He shook his head then opened the armoire where he'd placed some personal items. Even though they had a walk-in closet with enough space, Marco had preferred to keep some of his things locked. She doubted he suspected the housemaid would rob his stuff. Did he think she would?

She switched her weight from one foot to the other. *God, I hope not.* She loved him, which was completely outrageous, inconvenient, and unexpected, yet none of these arguments made it less true. What if he felt something for her, too? Maybe he didn't completely love her yet, but she'd seen the look in his eyes at the studio when she told him that sometimes plans changed and new goals came into view. Damn it, could she be so wrong?

I'll show him. She didn't have time on her side when it came to making him fall for her. She'd have to use her body to show him, without the words that would probably freak him out if she revealed just how much she cared for him. Perhaps the intensity of that emotion would be enough to convince him to give her a chance and forget about contracts.

He produced a black plastic bag and removed a box from it. "I want you to wear a dress, and underneath, this."

She tilted her head to the side, trying to register the shiny box with a red G-string inside. A couple of small devices were packed next to it: a black ring, and a—

"Is that a dildo?" she asked, grabbing the box from him.

Why, yes, it was. A small, round vibrator.

"This is a vibrating panty. You insert the vibrator in the slot," he said, pointing at the small opening on the interior lining of the underwear, exactly where it would cover her pussy.

Heat coiled low as she stared at the contents, fascinated, curious, and aroused. "This looks kinky."

He gave her a devastatingly sexy smile that weakened her knees and sent her pulse on a wild race. "Wear it tonight. This dildo has different settings, and I'll command it with my ring," he said, taking the ring from the box and sliding it on his finger.

"Are you serious?" The ring didn't give away its purpose, but simply had a couple of buttons on the side that she assumed he'd push to adjust the vibration settings.

Her clit throbbed, the idea sinfully wrong. "Why don't I wear the ring?"

"Because you won't make yourself come in public."

"You got that right," she said, feeling her cheeks burn. She wouldn't mind screwing him in public, as long as no one saw them. She didn't have the salaciousness to sweat in front of his family if she didn't have to. "I was going to take a shower. Wanna join me?" she asked.

"As much as I'd love to, no. I have some business emails I can't avoid. Take your shower, then put this on," he said, pointing at the box, "and get dressed."

"How long will I wear the panties?"

"Until tonight. I want you begging me to make you come by the time I take them off."

"Well, I have a request of my own, then. Tonight, I want us to go all the way," she said, as heat spread across her chest. She'd entertained the idea, and now, she was ready to try it with him. "I want you to take my ass."

Other than the butt plug they'd used, she'd never had anal sex before. Not full on, cock-in-her-ass sex. Hell, none of her boyfriends had even suggested it. They were too congenial, too sweet, too vanilla to entertain playing with her ass.

His gaze raked over her, pausing at her nipples then dipping lower still. When he lifted his eyes to meet hers, their chocolate depths smoldered with scorching promises. "It'll be my pleasure." He angled closer, erasing the inches between them.

"I want you to have me any way you can. I hope I won't let you down," she said. She'd hate to kill the mood by changing her mind at the last minute. A part of her, though, sizzled in anticipation to be claimed by him in the most primitive way a male could take a female. She'd fallen for him and yearned to give him every part of her.

"That would be impossible." He kissed her cheek, and the light brush of his lips on her skin nearly melted her bones.

• • •

I want you to have me any way you can.

Two hours later, Lily's words still haunted him. Marco drummed his fingers on the boat's railing, peering at all the villas and the mountains in the background but not really paying attention to any of it. If he closed his eyes, her image came to mind, and her startled gaze when he'd told her his plan.

Did she really want him, or was she fulfilling the contract? He looked down at the amber contents of his tumbler. He didn't have any doubt he excited her sexually—her body told him better than any heartfelt confession. But she also treated him with kindness, the way she'd been with those children earlier. Lily Jenkins was all future mother material.

Bringing their relationship to the basics, to the raw pull, was what he needed. That's why her suggestion to finally have anal sex came in handy. He'd have done it any other day, but tonight he needed it to show himself that the only thing holding them together was sex—raw, hot, temporary sex. He had to show her he'd never be a permanent fixture in her life. But was he doing it to protect himself, or her?

"Marco," Nico called him.

"Yeah?" He turned around, taking a drink of his scotch.

"Are you hiding?" Nico asked.

"That's not my style," Marco said. His grandmother had been talking to Lily for at least twenty minutes on the other side of the boat, and he'd decided to take a breather from the whole thing. His nonna apparently loved Lily, which had squeezed his heart. "What's up?"

"Look, man, I don't like to interfere, but you need to open your eyes. I don't think your so-called fiancée is who she says she is."

"Why not?"

"I never heard of a Patricia Doors before. I Googled her and couldn't find anything. Arietta told me earlier that she gave her some lousy excuse when she gave her a different name. Daisy or something. The name of a flower I think. Anyway, I'm worried you're so into this woman that you can't discern the truth."

"What's the truth, according to you?"

"She's a gold digger."

Marco threw his head back and laughed. He'd met his share of money-hungry women in his life, but Lily didn't fit the mold. Sure, she had agreed to his evil plan to bed her in exchange for what she wanted, but she wouldn't agree to marry someone unless she loved him. Unless it was a real marriage. That much he'd figured out. Which was why commitment between them would never work.

Nico frowned and glanced around as if to make sure no one heard him. "It's not funny. Are you serious about marrying her? You better consider a hell of a prenup to protect your assets. I bet this woman has been lying to you from the start."

"She got nervous. Everyone seems to be so interested in getting to know her, and Patricia never had this kind of attention before. It's intimidating."

"How long have you known her? This is so unlike you... to act so impulsively."

"Trust me," he said, squeezing his brother's shoulder.

Nico patted Marco's back. "I'll try."

"That's all I ask," he said, then waved at Nico. "Now, time to find her and make sure she hasn't changed her mind." With those words, he searched for Lily on the main deck, where his family members drank wine and told old stories. His father hadn't come to this activity, which was okay with him. The less he saw of him, the better.

He found his grandma moving to a song, smiling, her hands swaying from side to side as she kept up with the lyrics. Joy flooded his chest. He'd made the right decision in coming to the celebrations with Lily, his fake fiancée. Her presence distracted him from the lurking pain of how much he'd miss Nonna after she passed away. How much he already had missed her.

He scanned the area; no sign of Lily. Placing his tumbler on a console table, he kept walking until he spotted her on the other side of the deck, standing against the railing, looking at the lake. He rolled the side of the ring he was wearing, knowing it'd cause the dildo inside her pussy to vibrate.

He watched her, stalking closer, and gradually upped the intensity. She palmed the railing, her legs switching from side to side as if she fidgeted. His cock swelled upon that sight, his hands itching to touch her. He craved her in such a powerful way that he couldn't even articulate the words.

"Hi," he said softly, sandwiching her between the railing and himself.

She turned her head halfway. The nightly breeze ruffled the waves of her hair, and she tucked some of the loose strands behind her ear. "Hey."

"How are you doing, Lily?" He dipped his head to whisper her name in her ear.

"I..." She breathed. "I don't know how much longer I can take it. It's been inside me for too long, and recently it's started to vibrate."

He kissed her neck and outlined the side of her body with his hand. Everything about her was warm, soft, sexy. He rested his hand at her waist, his hand clenching on her, his fingers pressing into her skin. She moaned and planted both palms on the railing as if she needed the support.

His cock grew painfully hard. A rush of blood raced south in his body. He could take her to the bathroom and fuck her quickly, to give them both the release they'd been yearning.

"You're doing great," he said.

She clenched her thighs together, and he pressed his own between hers. "I'm so aroused I'm light-headed. I don't think I can carry a conversation or walk straight anymore."

Damn it. He didn't want her passing out on him. His blood pounded in his temples. He pulled her against him, his cock pressing against her. Because of his large frame, from afar, people wouldn't know what they were up to. He couldn't release himself, not yet, but if he wanted her to last tonight, he needed to help her now.

"Don't move," he said, and slid his finger on his ring, upping the vibration. Until then, he'd left it at the same rhythm, his idea to get her to simmer in a slow torture of libido.

"God," she hissed out. He looked down at her hands clasping the railing, her knuckles whitening.

"Come for me, baby. You need this now to prepare for what's happening later."

She rocked her hips against him, choking a gasp from

him. "I don't want to wait."

"You will." He snaked his hand to her breast and cupped it through the fabric of the forest-green dress. She leaned against him, molding so perfectly, he was the one getting dizzy with desire. "You'll do as I say. Tonight, I'll make you come like never before. I'll make sure you're desperate for my cock when I slam into your ass."

He felt the trembles washing over her body, his words alone provoking her. Then, he upped the level of his ring one more time. "Yes, *tesoro*, feel it." He slid his hand into her dress, and soon his finger teased her engorged nipple. She arched her back into him. "Give yourself to me, Lily. I want to take all of you later."

"Yes. Yes."

He pressed his ring to the maximum level and enjoyed seeing her jerk forward and backward, her breath growing heavier. She didn't say anything else, nor did she need to. He watched her, holding her, until she stopped quivering and turned to face him. Her face glowed, her eyes darkening. A shade of pink stained her cheeks. He turned off his vibrating ring, adamant on giving her some time to recover—after all, it'd be a long night.

Chapter Thirteen

"Where do you think you're going?" Arietta asked Lily when she left the deck.

Lily curled her fingers into a ball. After the fabulous cruise on the Lake and the orgasm from an hour ago, she could do without small talk. "It's been a long day. I'm going to bed," she said. Marco had been with her until a few minutes ago, when his uncle had called him over to talk about his grandmother's health. At least, that's what Marco had told her—she assumed whenever they exchanged words in Italian, they didn't want her to know.

"I understand. Can I walk up with you to the mansion? I'd like to have a few words with you."

Oh, shit. "Sure."

She strolled alongside Arietta who, despite her height and long legs, marched in tandem with her. Apprehension skated up Lily's throat, suffocating her. What if Arietta had figured out who she really was? Things were going so well, what with Marco's grandma really believing their story. *So well, I even fell for it.* Her heart skipped a beat.

A number of guests waited for the shuttle that would take them back to the mansion. Given her heels, Lily chastised herself for not getting in the shuttle. "I have to tell Marco where I am."

"Already done. I asked my husband to let him know. Come."

Lily stomped onto the stony ground. "What is it?" she asked. Best to put all cards on the table now.

"You surprised me, Patricia. Not a lot of people do, and I wanted to make sure I told you so."

Lily folded her arms, unsure if Arietta had given her a compliment or an insult.

Arietta's facial expressions softened. "When I saw you last night, I won't lie, I was worried. Besides being ridiculously handsome, my cousin is also filthy rich. I didn't want you to be interested in his money or what he can provide for your career."

Lily took in a deep breath, letting it out slowly. She unfolded her arms, unsure what to do or say. She was no gold digger, but part of what Arietta feared was true—she had a financial gain from the situation, even if she had used her body as currency. "I understand," she said in a low voice. Words to defend herself faltered her.

"I was wrong," Arietta said, and Lily raised her gaze to hers. "I know you care about my cousin. I saw the way you looked at him today. Reminds me of me when I met my husband."

"I do," Lily said, her voice trembling with emotion. Confiding in anyone at this point gave her so much relief. She wanted to shout out her feelings for him but knew she couldn't—not when he wasn't ready to learn about them.

"I know. He needs that, you know. He may be all strong and powerful, but inside he's got a few broken pieces."

"Yeah, his father doesn't seem overexcited to see him,

either," she said, making an effort not to spill any of the family history Marco had told her.

"Uncle Calogero has his flaws, but he's old school. He thinks staying away is best. God, are you sure you want to join this family?"

"Nobody is perfect."

"That's true. But when you see your mother kill herself in front of you as a child...you can't expect much normalcy as an adult."

Lily stopped on her heels. "He was there?"

"Oh *cazzo*. You didn't know? Yes. He was there."

Tears pricked at the corner of her eyes, but she blinked them back. The image of a scared little boy watching his mother take her own life stabbed at her mind. She shook her head. If she let herself go there, if she simply mused over the pain that he'd carried all those years, she wouldn't move forward. She wouldn't be able to be his tonight.

Sex wouldn't cure him. Sex wasn't the direct answer. But if she gave all she had, if she showed him with her body how much she trusted him, hopefully one day he'd trust her in return. He'd open his heart to her and receive all she wanted to give him.

. . .

Marco closed the door behind him. The downside of avoiding most of his Italian family members for so long was having to catch up with them all at once in a matter of days. His uncle Benicio had lured him into the conversation about his grandmother's health then had switched the conversation over to the stock market and asked for Marco's business advice.

He was about to switch on the light when he realized there were candles spread throughout the room. Curious, he kept walking until he reached Lily, who sat in the middle of the bed wearing the corset he'd brought her. When he made the purchase, his mouth watered at the thought of her luscious body in the fuchsia garment. Her high cleavage nearly spilled from the bust, and a hint of her aureoles peeked over the edge. The hourglass figure–hugging fabric outlined her tight nipples perfectly. He grew hard, his cock straining against his pants. Fucking right move buying the corset. The reality of seeing Lily in the sexy lingerie surpassed his fantasy.

"I hope you don't mind me breaking into your little toy box," she said, turning her head in the direction of the armoire where he'd hidden his purchases. "I got here early, showered, and thought, hmmm…how can I fill my time until my man gets here?"

My man. He liked the sound of that, a little too much. Grinning, he removed his jacket and placed it on the tufted chair in front of the vanity dresser. "You almost gave your man a heart attack."

"Good." She moved her body, swiveling around to show him her lack of underwear. "I hope this is okay." She spread her legs apart, giving him a full view of her soaking wet pussy.

More heat slammed into his groin. She was so hot, so ready. For him. Only him. He shook his head. She was wet, poised for him to take her in any way, because he'd gotten her there with those sexy panties, making her come before he took what he wanted tonight, nothing more.

He unbuttoned his shirt, finding it more difficult with each button. She chuckled at his desperation, but he didn't care. Keeping his eyes on hers, he pulled down his slacks and boxer briefs. When they pooled at his feet, he removed his socks and shoes. His hard-on sprung free, and he squeezed the tip of his cock in an attempt to calm himself down.

He wanted her to savor every part of being taken by him from behind. And for that to happen, she needed to be pleasured without rush. "It's more than okay." He studied the room and found a textured vibrator and a tube of lubricant on the nightstand next to the bed. "Though, you were a bad girl for going through my box of toys."

"I was?"

"Yes. And bad girls need to be punished."

Her lips parted. He sat on the edge of the bed and crooked his finger. "Come here. I'll teach you not to do it again."

She got on her hands and knees and moved on the bed with the elegance of a cat. Little charges of electricity kept searing his insides, each time more strongly. He had to really focus not to have her simply suck him straight away.

"Where do you want me, Big Daddy?"

"Lay with your tummy down and your ass on my lap."

She did as told, and he caught a whiff of her magnificent perfume blended with a remarkable scent of female arousal. He inhaled, wanting to taste her. He'd get to it soon. Now he had to enjoy her willingness to play along.

She adjusted herself on him, and pre-cum bubbled at the tip of his cock, the pressure building inside. He flattened her with his hand, stroking her smooth back, then made invisible circles on her large, perky butt cheeks until her flesh warmed under his touch. she moaned, warning him she liked what he did to her.

He'd always taken charge in sexual relations, but he'd never taken it this far. With Lily, he could. Despite what had brought them together, she wouldn't judge him. She allowed him to be in control, even though he felt like an impostor. The ruthless force of desire commanded him, and he acted as a mere executioner.

"You shouldn't play with my toys when I'm not around."

"I'm sorry. I wanted to surprise you."

He palmed her delicious ass, loving the feel of her muscly cheek. Then he swatted it.

She gasped, moving, and he waited for a sign to make sure he could proceed. His last intention was to hurt her. Soon, she popped her ass up again, squirming, a sign she was ready for more. It seemed like the same force that guided him had taken over her as well. Was it just desire, though? Could it be something—

Before he mused on nonsense, he smacked her ass again, the sound louder this time. God, Lily was so hot. He pulled her hair a little bit, making her turn her face and see him. "Maybe you did this because you wanted to be punished. You like to play dirty, don't you, Lily? Or should I say Patricia?" Since they were role playing, might as well give her another name. Patricia… Someone who had it together in the boardroom but kissed any inhibitions goodbye in the bedroom.

"Yes, Big Daddy, I do."

"Dirty is the only way to play." He swatted her ass again, her skin warmer, a shade of red spreading through her cheek. "I have plans for your ass, so I don't want to hurt it too much. Not yet." He gave her one last smack; this time she moaned louder.

To soothe her, he massaged her cheeks until she squirmed, moving her head from side to side, her hair a gorgeous swish of blond. *Dio.* This woman was like a weapon created to destroy him. If his enemies heard of her, they'd use her to decipher corporate secrets and bring him to his ultimate downfall. What a sweet death it'd be.

He nudged her thighs apart and slipped his finger into her pussy. The drenching wet walls squeezed him, her inner muscles clinging to him. "I need to eat you. Turn around."

"What if I want you in my mouth, too?"

A smile curled at his lips. "Scoot up on the bed."

Within a few seconds, he covered her with his body, his head buried in her twat as she took his cock into her mouth. Being on top offered the perfect fit for his cock. He could fuck her mouth good and move his legs.

He licked her walls, teased her clit, and worked in a frantic way to taste her, to devour her, to make her come undone for him. He sought the evidence she was in this as much as he was. The fact that he needed her scared the hell out of him, so at least knowing he wasn't alone encouraged him. Her moans filled the room, combined with little growls of pleasure.

As retaliation, she took him into her mouth with intent. She played with his hard, tingly balls as she sucked him up and down, her tongue fetching the little drops of pre-cum that spilled from his tip. "If you keep going like this, I won't last long," he said, coming out from between her legs a second.

She responded by claiming his dick completely, taking him in and out of her mouth, teasing him like the little minx she was. He intensified the flicks on her clit, sucking her deep like he wanted a part of her to enter him and never leave. "Oh. I'm, I'm coming..." she said, and he inserted a finger in her butt as she shook under him, calling his name before taking him back in her mouth and sucking him hard.

Strands of pleasure built in his core, brewed at the pit of his stomach, and made their way down a lot quicker than he would have wanted. He let out a groan or two. With one hand, she held his cock so she could deep throat him and suck all she could handle. He never expected to fully fit in a woman's mouth, but fuck, she was really trying. With the other hand, she gave his achy balls one last squeeze, then her palm slid down his thigh. She picked up the pace, and he felt a part of him throbbing against her throat. To make matters worse, or in this case better, she stroked his inner thigh, a place she had never attempted to play with before. Was she—

"Yes," he hissed out as she inserted two fingers into his hole, and soon his words broke in his throat. Coming undone, he exploded inside her mouth, strong, warm, and utterly defeated.

Chapter Fourteen

Lily didn't know how long she'd waited for her breathing to ease down. She looked at the ceiling, with Marco next to her. They'd both come in each other's mouths, and an immense satisfaction filled her.

"So you have a couple of tricks of your own," he said, breaking the soothing silence.

She slanted her face in his direction. "Was it wrong?" She'd read in an old sex article in a magazine about how women drove men crazy in a certain area of their anatomy. She'd never been bold enough to try it before she met Marco.

He stroked her cheek, and she leaned into his caress. "You're one of a kind, Lily. If me exploding in your mouth wasn't enough of an answer, I don't know what else to say."

She had to smile. "Good."

She kissed the back of his hand, and her clit throbbed, warning her it was ready for more fun. Encouraged, she took one of his fingers into her mouth and sucked it, nibbled on it, brought it into her mouth just like she had with his gorgeous cock.

"You're a natural born cocksucker. How did I get so lucky?"

She drove his finger, glistening with her saliva, down her body, then placed it on her hardening nipple. "You bring out the worst in me."

"I say the same thing," he said, then lunged on top of her, overwhelming her with his large frame. She arched toward him, needing his warm form to envelop her. He sucked on her breast while his hand cupped the other, pinching her nipple. She linked her legs around his torso, so happy in latching onto him.

He alternated tits, and she murmured his name countless times, like the entrancing lyric of a song. She clenched her legs tighter around him, already needing him inside her badly. "Marco, please." Her pussy throbbed for him.

She slid her hand down and fisted his rod, reveling in how hard it already was and earning a growl from him. Her eagerness had the opposite effect, for he disengaged from her. She eyed him with disappointment, about to protest, when a devilish grin spread across his face.

"Turn around and get on all fours for me."

She gathered whatever strength she had left in her and obeyed his demand, her palms and toes on the mattress. He grabbed the dildo she'd put on the nightstand, and also the small bottle of lube. She watched him bring them close and put them next to him. He positioned himself behind her ass, and she looked down at the pillow, in a mix of excitement and apprehension. What if she sucked at this? She'd done so well tonight bringing new things to the table—her table, anyway. She doubted there was much she could do to him he hadn't done before. But she refused to overanalyze it.

She heard him open the bottle and squirt some liquid in his hand. Soon, he massaged the area between her cheeks, splitting them apart as his finger spread the lube. What she hadn't counted on was the lube warming her skin and awakening her nerve endings. A world of sensations opened itself to her, and she swayed, aroused.

He splayed his hand on her lower back, steadying her. His touch staked a claim, his hand strong and powerful. She enjoyed the sensation of him taking charge more than words could describe. He spread her thighs with his leg and started to play with her sex.

She gasped, loving him teasing her walls, her skin down there still sensitized after the orgasm, after he had eaten her like she was an exquisite dish for a starving man. She felt something playing with her entrance, the tip teasing her clit.

The dildo. The texture was different than his, a tad rougher.

"Relax, *tesoro*. You'll enjoy this, I promise. I'm going to play with your pussy and penetrate you with this. Then, when you're about to burst from pleasure, I'll fuck your ass until we're both spent."

She looked over her shoulder and saw his eyes darkening to a matte black. He'd never looked so intense and hot. "I trust you. Fuck my ass, Big Daddy," she said, calling the nickname she probably would never use again, but it made sense for their crazy role play game.

"Is your ass ready?"

"Yes."

"I'll make it mine. Thanks for saving it for me," he said, and began working her with the dildo. She bucked backward, her limbs almost bending from the delightful frisson traveling through her.

"Feels so good. Not as good as you, but I like it because you're the one doing it."

He thrust the dildo in and out of her, and she choked out her moans. At some point, she felt like an animal, a primal being outside her body. All the emotions assailed her, fogging her mind so the only thing in it, the only thing that made sense, was him.

"Oh, yes. Yes. I'm getting so close already," she said.

"Me, too. I need to come inside of you, baby. I need to feel you."

"Come inside me. Please. I need you in me."

He poked her entrance with the tip of his cock, also using his finger to stretch her, like he had when he'd used the butt plug. Maybe to distract her, he pumped his dildo in and out of her with a crazy rhythm. Pleasure fogged her brain, and she quivered, the climax drilling her from top to bottom.

He advanced the stake of his claim, his cock entering her tight channel. She convulsed, her pussy nearly destroyed, but he didn't stop ramming it with the dildo. "Marco... Marco... This is too much... I'm about to die."

"No, baby. You're going to keep coming."

She mellowed. She turned around to see him and found him sweaty, smiling victoriously, his cock halfway into her. Fuck, he was having the time of his life. "Come all the way, babe."

"Oh, yes," he said, and thrust his dick inside her. She gasped, trying to get used to his girth and size. It had taken her pussy a while to get used to him—she barely had been able to fit him completely when she'd deep throated him, so now she clung onto the pleasure he gave her, teasing her pussy, and relaxed her hips so he could impale her ass.

"I never... I never did this without a condom before. I can't wait to fill your sweet ass with my cum and see it drip from your thighs."

His dirty talking pushed her over the brink, and she let go again, riding that damn dildo relentlessly until it hit a spot inside her and she screamed his name. Her world shattered into countless pieces, and she had not an ounce of energy left in her. She dropped her hands down. Her face, drenched in sweat, hit the softness of the pillows.

He removed his hand from her, taking away the sticky vibrator. He perched his hands on her sides. As her last conscious act, she rocked her hips into him, locking him deep inside her, giving him the go-ahead for continuing the search for his own apex.

He retreated from her only to return again, so deeply that her head moved. Soon, his thrusts quickened, and she heard his breath heaving, her brain still barely able to assimilate much beyond the amazing climax she'd just experienced. When he released himself into her, he produced a manly, coarse sound that prickled her skin.

He filled her hole with his warm seed until he eased off of her and dropped to her side.

A silence stretched between them. They glanced at each other, and she had to swallow to keep from shouting the words begging for a release of their own.

"How are you doing?" he asked.

"Blissfully exhausted. You?"

"Satisfied like never before." He scooted closer and kissed her forehead. "You're amazing, Lily. I'll never forget… tonight."

She snuggled up to him, and he held her, planting gentle kisses on her shoulder. "Neither will I."

• • •

The next three days, they decided to hang out by the pool and spend time with his grandmother in the afternoons. After five exquisite nights, they had only one more day in Italy before heading back to the States. Marco's heart did a silly flip whenever Lily looked at him, the memories of the previous night still burning in his mind.

Even now, as she talked to his grandmother over tea and biscuits on the outdoor terrace, he had difficulty shoving the images away. Lily was always so responsive, so vibrant, scorching in his hands.

"Marco. Marco," his grandmother called him.

He blinked. "Yes?"

"Get the bag behind you, please," she said, pointing at the

gift bag on the chair next to him. She'd appeared downstairs carrying it, and he'd assumed she brought a gift to Lily.

He'd been right. Nonna took it from him, glanced at the bag lovingly, then with a sigh, handed it to Lily.

"I want you to have it," she said.

"Thank you, but you didn't have to get me anything," Lily said, removing the tissue paper. When she produced a velvet box, her eyes widened. She opened it to find a glorious necklace filled with diamonds and peppered with emeralds.

Marco's throat thickened. He recognized the lavish jewelry, despite not seeing it for many years.

"This belonged to my daughter. Since you're marrying my grandson, I'd like for you to have it," Nonna said.

Lily parted her lips, but hesitated. She petted the necklace, her fingers tracing the diamonds that sparkled in response. Quickly, she closed the box. "I–I can't take it. I mean, I'm flattered you're giving it to me, but it's too big of a gift. It should stay in the family."

"You will. You're joining the family, aren't you?"

"Yes."

"Then what's keeping you from accepting?"

Lily glanced at him, the look in her eyes a plea for him to try to change his grandmother's mind. "It's so beautiful."

"She'll take it," Marco said, covering her hand with his.

"Thank you very much," Lily said at last. "I never had something so special."

His heart shrank to the size of a pebble. God, what was she saying? She should be showered with the most exotic jewelry. By him.

"My daughter would have loved you, Lily. You're so open and kind. I'm thankful my grandson has found you."

A rolling sensation unsettled his stomach. He loved his nonna and appreciated her positivity. The mother he remembered had a hard time connecting with him, let alone someone he brought for her to meet. Growing up, he never had playdates with boys his age, always hanging with Nico and his friends. His father could have interfered, could have been more present, but had cowardly chosen not to. He thinned his lips to keep from saying anything.

A tear rolled down Lily's cheek, and she wiped it with the back of her hand. "Me, too," she said hoarsely, as if the words got trapped in her throat.

"If you'll excuse me, the excitement of the festivities is making me tired. Thank you for the chat," his grandmother said, gesturing for her nurse, who rushed to assist her and take her to her room.

Lily clasped her hands together. "Wow."

"What?"

"Can't you see the irony? Your grandma wants me to have this so she'll keep the necklace in the family. And the whole reason I came here was that I wanted to keep the salon in my family. We have something in common."

"Yes."

She flashed him an apologetic smile. "Listen, she's being amazingly generous, but I won't keep this. I'll give it to you. She'll think I kept it, and you can do whatever you want with it. Maybe sell it and donate the money to a worthy cause. This necklace is worth a lot. It could change the life of some homeless folks."

"Why are you so selfless?" he asked. Couldn't she just accept the gift?

"Ugh, I'm not Mother Teresa."

"No, but compared to some of the people I know, you're the next best thing," he said, then he rose to his feet, needing to move around to clear his head.

"Is this about your mother?"

He pinched the bridge of his nose. "How do you know?"

"You seemed uneasy when your grandmother mentioned her."

He waved her off then turned around to face the lake. "My mother was sick. It wasn't her fault," he said.

Lily wasn't going to let him off so easily. She neared him until they stood side by side, staring at his profile. "I understand. A lot of people are sick these days."

He swallowed the bile in the back of his throat. He locked his spine, already regretting what he was about to say. What good was it to hide it at this point? The trip brought up his past in more ways than one, and Lily sensed his reactions even when he tried so hard to hide them. She'd earned the right to know.

"Her death was my fault."

"What do you mean?"

He looked at her. God. She'd hate him when she found out the truth. "When my mother died…"

She placed her hand over his. "You were there. I know. It's okay."

Marco jerked away from her, his blood pressure spiking. Surprise shook him. How much did she know? "Who told you?"

Apparently unfazed, Lily didn't move an inch. She gave him a once-over and straightened her shoulders. "Your cousin," she said softly, almost as if she wished she didn't have to reveal it to him.

He didn't need to ask which one. He thrust his fingers into his hair, wishing for an instant Arietta were a male. "Well, you won't think it's okay when I finish telling you the truth. You'll want to break the deal, or you'll hate me."

"Don't you think I can make that decision by myself?"

"My mother is dead…and I killed her," he said the words evenly, remembering the pain in his father's eyes the moment he came home and found the blood soaking the carpet. Marco's heart raced, just like his legs had when his father had shouted, several times. He'd gone to find his nanny for some comfort.

He doubted after tonight Lily would be interested in comforting him—sexually or otherwise.

Chapter Fifteen

"What?" she asked, crossing her arms like a chilly wind had slapped her in the face. Might as well have. She shook her head, registering what she'd heard. "How did it happen?"

"My birth triggered her disease. My father always resented me for it, and you know some of the story. Before her death, she was having a hard time again. She'd been between medicines. Some of them made her very groggy. She slept a lot during the day and stayed up at night. Sometimes, Nico and I didn't see her for days."

He massaged his temples quickly, like he wanted to will away a migraine. "I blamed her. I couldn't connect with her, even though I wanted to, so much. Whenever I wished I had a normal mother, I felt guilty for even thinking that way."

She stretched out her hand to touch his, but he moved a couple of feet away from her. Sadness at what he'd experienced blended with a building frustration. How come his father had encouraged that crazy train of thought, possibly even instilled it in him? "You were just a kid."

"When she found the gun from my father's collection, I

saw her walking around with it. I called her, and she came into my room."

The look he gave her was pure torture. Her spine stiffened, and her breath caught in her dry throat. "What did you do?"

His hands curled into fists. She didn't try to hold him, just listened, motionless. "Nothing. I could have run and told someone. I could have screamed. I could even have convinced her not to pull that trigger. But I watched her, without saying a word. She stared at me quietly, the haunted look in her eyes so raw. Maybe she found it easier to do it there, right in front of me. She killed herself, and I was her accomplice."

"Did you freeze?" she managed to ask in a steady voice. The heartbreak behind his words made complete sense. Her chest clutched, and she had to smooth her hands on her dress to keep from reaching out to him again. Damn it.

"Yes. In a way, that part of me is still frozen. It's better this way. When I tried to unfreeze it once, didn't work out too well."

"Is that why your fiancée ended the engagement?"

"I told her what happened, and she couldn't handle it. I understand. It's not as if, were we to have kids, we would have a warm grandfather on my side."

She shook her head, wishing, for the first time in her life, to bitch-slap someone. "She was a superficial idiot."

"She wasn't ready to handle a guy like me. She was nice. And sweet…much like you."

Anger welled up inside. Anger at his father, at his past circumstances…and anger at the woman who didn't see through him. "Don't you dare compare me to someone who runs when the going gets tough," she said, enunciated each word carefully to make sure he heard them.

He inched closer. "I didn't mean to hurt you," he said gently.

She lifted her chin, adamant on not backing down. "I'm not hurt. Just setting things straight."

A sweet smile formed on his lips. "You're cute when you're angry."

She rolled her eyes. "Whatever. It's your life, but if you want to be mad at someone, be mad at your father for not being there for you when you needed him. For blaming you because of his own poor parenting skills."

"Trust me, I am." The vein in his neck pulsed. His eyes darkened with resentment. "Why do you think we don't have a relationship?"

"Then why can't you move past your mother's suicide?" she asked, then realized she'd almost shouted her question. She took a long, sharp intake of breath. "I mean…er… I'm asking as a friend. I know our situation is temporary, but you're a tremendous guy with a lot to give. Do you want to have arrangements like ours for the rest of your life?"

"What is marriage but an arrangement?"

"You're wrong. Marriage is so much more than that. It's two souls, two real people choosing to be together through thick and thin. People who pick each other because of both their qualities and flaws," she said with every ounce of pride she could afford. Her parents' marriage taught her not to settle for less than what they'd shared.

Marco stared at her in silence, with hooded eyes, and she'd give anything to know what went on in his mind. He probably thought she was a naive, idealistic girl who knew nothing about the world. She snorted, knowing she needed to cool down before continuing the argument. *Maybe he isn't ready to hear it all. Maybe he'll be able to experience that kind of love, to witness it one day if he's lucky.*

"Listen, I'm going upstairs for a little bit. I need to call my mom. I haven't talked to her in a couple of days, and she'll worry if I disappear. Excuse me."

. . .

"How are you enjoying your vacation, dear?" her mother asked. She'd fed her some bullshit about winning a ticket in a contest to attend a European tradeshow.

"It's great," she said, injecting enthusiasm into her voice and hoping she pulled it off. There wouldn't be enough time in a confessional chair for all the lies she'd been telling. She should text, but after the discussion with Marco, she needed to talk to someone, even if the subject didn't involve him or his disturbing father. "I miss you."

"I miss you, too, honey, but it's only a week, right? You'll be home soon. I can't wait to hear all your news. Are you making a lot of friends?"

Her lips broke into a smile. "Mom, this isn't summer camp."

"I know, but who said work can't be fun, too? I've always wanted to visit Italy. I heard Italian men are good-looking hunks. Have you met any of those?"

"Oh, trust me, I have. He's hunky, all right." She snickered, knowing full well her mother and her friends would drop their jaws if they ever saw Marco.

"Then good for you. Enjoy, sweetie. Life's not just work and no play."

She talked to her mother for a few more minutes, and the apprehension that had built in her chest eased. Her mother's voice always had the power to soothe her, even if she knew damn well it'd only be temporary.

After she hung up the phone, she lay on the bed, looking at the textured ceiling. She heard the door open but refused to look at Marco. She could feel his presence, the way he strode intently into the room. Maybe he didn't want to chat with her, either. She was supposed to be a modern-day concubine, and she'd pushed him to discuss a subject he clearly hated.

Well, whatever. Despite her contractual obligations, there was only so much pretending she could handle. She kept gazing upward, her intertwined hands on her stomach.

She heard him opening the armoire, and a few seconds later, felt the weight of his body on the mattress. Did he expect her to have sex with him now, when she was confused, overwhelmed, and possibly upset?

"It's not who am I underneath, but what I do that defines me." Was he quoting a Batman movie?

She gave in and glanced to her right, finding Marco wearing a black mask of Batman. She'd seen it once, briefly, when she'd looked into the bag the previous day. Before their anal extravaganza.

She sat on the bed. "Batman?" she asked, studying how the mask conveniently left his mouth and cheeks free.

"I Googled the quote. Thought you'd like it."

A silly bubble of happiness burst inside her. "Nice try. Is that all you have to say?"

"I know you meant well, Lily. It may seem I'm not as open to you as you'd like, but I'm more open with you than I am with anyone else. I appreciate you not running away…at least, not any farther than our bedroom." He tucked a strand of hair behind her ear.

She narrowed her eyes at him. "I needed a breather."

"I know. I was teasing you."

She outlined his lips with her finger, and a thrill of excitement shot up her arm. "Why aren't you used to people sticking up for you? Your brother seems invested. So does your grandma."

"Nowadays, everyone wants something. It's easier when you know their goal than when you have to entertain ideas about what they want."

"Spoken like a true cynic."

He nibbled her finger. "A cynic who wants to show you

how grateful he is for all the sticking up you've been doing."

"I wonder how he'd do such thing."

He splayed his strong hand on her stomach, thrusting her down on the bed. Then he covered her body with his. "I've heard you're hiding a special kind of weapon, in liquid form, that can kill the entire world's population. It's my duty, as protector of Gotham, to search for it by all means necessary."

"I'll never tell," she said, joining in the role-playing game. "I've worked too hard to be where I am today. You should know something about hardship," she said, sliding her hand down until she caressed his cock through his pants. "You have a weapon of your own."

"Yeah, and I'm not afraid to use it."

GOOD. She bit her lips to keep from shouting.

He grabbed her wrist and jerked it away from him, making it clear he was in control. Damn it, if pleasure was her outcome, he could take charge any day. Besides, how else would they save humanity?

Marco opened the buttons of her dress and fumbled with her bra until her nipples popped out. He dipped his head and licked one taut bud, sending a trail of tingles through her all the way to her pussy. Her folds slicked and swelled, the idea of him being inside again tempting.

She bucked into him, already wanting to offer herself. He gave a hearty chuckle against her skin, no doubt reading her mind. He sucked on the other breast until she moaned, then headed south for more exploration.

He slid his fingers into her underwear. "I found the weapon. Now I must drain it, to make sure you won't use it against anyone."

"What if I use it against you?"

He put his fingers at each side of her underwear, then ripped it apart. "Oh, I can take it."

• • •

Marco tossed her panties aside. The unique aroma of her delicious pussy swirled into his nostrils, and he inhaled it with gusto. He parted her wet folds, her sex so ready for him, her walls swollen, her clit nicely engorged. He stared at it for a moment, fascinated. "Looking at you makes me thirsty," he said gruffly.

"Then drink up, Batman. Gotham can't wait forever."

"Neither can I."

He lowered his head, positioning himself in between her thighs so he could lick her all he wanted, but keeping his eyes on hers. He wanted to see all of her reactions, to record that memory in his mind. Forever.

He thrust two fingers inside her, and her inner walls clung to him, squeezing him. She watched him, and for a moment that stretched beyond belief, their gazes held. His cock grew so hard, and pre-cum rose at the tip. How gorgeous was she? Lily. His Lily.

"Yes, oh yes. Touch me. I like when you touch me."

He teased her with his tongue, lapping at her clit until she squirmed into his mouth and at last broke their stare. He added another finger to this relentless quest, quickening his rhythm in her flesh.

For the next few minutes, he provoked her, sucking her clit, licking her walls, finger fucking her soaked pussy. Each time he licked her, his heart thrummed louder than before, his own body sending him warning signals. She shook, the spasms claiming her. He kept a close watch on her, enjoying the lovely view of his woman coming undone.

"God."

He disengaged from between her legs, and he was about to surge to his feet, when she asked, "Where are you going?"

He hadn't meant to make this about him. Sure, she

probably saw his hard-on protesting the confines of his pants. But he had wanted to make her climax because that was the only thing he could give her. She hadn't run like Angelica—even though a tiny voice reminded him she'd been paid to be loyal, to be in his bed. He preferred to believe Lily rose above all that. She was different.

"I don't want you to think you need to do anything. This was about you."

"Great, so it can still be about me if you fuck me silly in this bed. Unless, of course, you're not interested," she said sweetly.

Not interested? He'd be a dead man before he was not interested.

He took off his shirt, pulled down his shorts and boxers. She sat on the bed, her breasts spilling from her bra but not completely free; her hair messy, her face flushed. He almost wished he could freeze that moment forever.

For the second time today, that word haunted him—forever wasn't part of the plan. Despite her politically correct spiel about accepting him the way he was, with the family he had, he knew, in the long-haul, things would change.

Until they did…he'd take her for as long as he could.

Chapter Sixteen

The day of Nonna's party had arrived. Because of Lily by his side, he'd almost forgotten his purpose in coming on this trip—to bid his grandmother farewell, even if she refused to discuss her health.

Marco had spoken to the cousins who had accompanied Nonna to her doctor's appointment and exams, and they guaranteed him she was good enough to be part of the celebrations as long as she remembered her limitations and weak heart. She dressed to the nines and smiled, but she always had a nurse close by, and she usually retired from the festivities much earlier than anyone else.

The weight of a grand piano sat on his chest. He'd miss her, even if he hadn't been around much in the past years. Seeing her always put a smile on his face.

"Arietta asked me to help her with her dress when I'm ready," Lily said to him. "Is it okay if we meet downstairs?" A deep green gown outlined her delectable curves.

"I would prefer to crease your dress before," he said, embracing her, his hand sliding down to caress her ass.

She nudged his elbow and jerked away from him. "Nope. Tonight is the last opportunity I'll have to look like I'm attending a red-carpet event, and you're not ruining it, mister."

Though her voice was amused, he tensed up. She had a point. The next morning, they'd travel back to the States, where he only had one more week left with her.

"I'll ruin the dress later," he said, pulling her to him.

She kissed his cheek. "The dress and the makeup. Not now."

Before he caught her mouth with his, she pushed him away with a mischievous grin and sashayed out of the room.

He buttoned up his immaculate white shirt and was about to search for the rest of his tuxedo hanging in the closet, when someone knocked on the door. "Come in," he said.

Elegantly dressed, Nico marched into the room. "I just ran into *Lily* in the hallway, so I thought I'd come in and talk to you."

Marco grabbed the jacket and slid it on. "Shoot," he said.

Nico paced in a small circle until he stopped, staring at him square in the eye. "I just called her Lily, Marco. Not Patricia. I know the truth."

Marco paused for an instant. His neck stiffened; his jaw clenched. If he made a big deal, Nico would go for blood. Instead, he decided to act as natural as possible. Ignoring the chill moving through his veins, he turned to his brother and adjusted his sleeves. "So?"

Nico's dark green eyes glared. "So? She's lying to all of us, and you're in on it. Are you insane?"

"No. It's my life, and I don't owe you any explanations."

Nico shook his head. "Yes, you do. You can screw whoever you want—I'm not a saint myself. That said, when we have to back off a huge deal because she doesn't want to sell her precious shop, then yeah, we have a problem."

Marco took the tie and began to loop it around his neck. His brother had a point. He had to give him some explanation because they did business together. Besides, if he got him in his corner, if he made him understand, maybe he wouldn't spill the beans to anyone, and the dirty little secret would never make its way to their grandmother.

"Sit down. I'll tell you."

Nico gestured with his hands. "I'm too pumped to sit."

"I brought Lily here because I wanted to show Nonna I've found someone, as my parting gift for her. Our engagement isn't real, but I want to keep that information private. Nonna always wanted me to find someone."

Nico rolled his eyes, shaking his head. "Yeah, you were always her favorite."

Marco thinned his lips. Arguing that statement was beneath him, because it had always been true. Nonna loved all her grandchildren but favored Marco many times, trying to compensate for the tragic loss of their mother and the absence of his father. "I needed her the most."

Nico jammed his hand into his suit then leaned against the doorjamb. They never dwelled on the past much, and Marco preferred it that way. Why worry about what couldn't change? "You didn't tell me because I'd do the math and know who she was."

"Yeah."

"Why Lily, though? I mean she's gorgeous, got a fabulous rack—"

Marco lifted his hand in objection. "You better stop right there, brother. Don't talk about her that way."

Nico gave him a slow nod, his brows furrowing like he was trying hard to understand. What was there to grasp? The situation was quite simple, actually. "How did this whole thing happen?" Nico asked. "Did she ask you to quit trying to buy her salon? How about her bills?"

"I paid them." He'd signed a contract to take care of half of them upon her signature and the other half at the end of their contract. Five days ago, he'd emailed his lawyer and asked him to use his power of attorney and pay the remaining debt. It'd be one less thing to worry about when the time came to say goodbye to Lily.

"You paid them," Nico said, running a hand down his face. "Of course you did."

Why did his brother mock him like he was some kind of stupid fool? He felt like a geeky kid with a crush on the cheerleader. "It's between me and her. I forbid you to mention any of this to her or anyone else. We know gossip runs like wildfire in this family, and I don't want Nonna to find out. It won't be good for her, which would defeat the whole purpose."

"Don't worry, Marco. Your secret is safe with me."

"Thank you."

"You fell for her, didn't you?"

Marco frowned. "Excuse me?"

"You were always fond of your little contracts or fuck agreements. You always made sure women wouldn't screw you over after the affair ended. Confidentiality agreement, all that show," Nico said. "The old Marco would never let a woman come between him and his work."

Marco's heart heaved. His brother had completely lost it. He hadn't fallen for Lily. He ran his fingers through his hair, searching for an appropriate way to say he'd purchased her heavenly pussy for the month. "I can't tell you all the details of our deal, but I guarantee you I don't love her," he said, and for some odd reason his voice lost energy at the end, the thickness in his throat making it hard to choke out the words.

Nico chuckled. "Listen, you don't have to worry. I won't tell anyone. You know… I've seen how you look at her. Hell, you almost punched me for mentioning her breasts a few seconds ago, when in the past you wouldn't even care if I dated someone you had screwed."

Marco plopped on the bed, defeated like someone just told him his dog had died. Couldn't be. "Lily is different. I enjoy being with her. I'm addicted to her, but that's the extent of it," he said out loud, unsure if to himself or his brother.

Nico sat next to him and patted his back. "It's okay, bro. Zaine got married. Now you. I need to watch out for the signs, so I can skip the same doomed fate."

Married? Marco snorted. No wonder he'd never told his brother about their deal. Nico enjoyed twisting facts to his advantage. "We aren't getting married."

Nico tapped his back, consoling him. "Sure."

Marco jerked away and rose to his feet. Enough mockery. "It's not funny. Get out," he said, pointing toward the door.

Nico stood and made his way out, keeping a smile on his face that Marco felt like punching away. *Idiota.* His brother knew nothing about him, Lily, or what went on between them.

. . .

"Happy Birthday, Debora," Lily said to his grandmother, gently kissing her cheek. She'd bought a small gift in town in the morning, which she'd added to the mountain of presents at the table. The party organizer had done an amazing job. Pictures of each decade of Nonna's life had been enlarged and displayed on stands across the living room. Even though Lily guessed about eighty guests were in attendance, the soft lighting and textured drapes smoothed the ambience and gave it a quainter atmosphere.

"Thank you, dear. It's 'Nonna' for you. After all, you're about to become family."

Lily managed a smile and allowed the person next to her to greet Nonna. She'd been downstairs for one hour, and still no sign of Marco. How long did it take him to get ready?

During the past few days, she'd grown used to watching him shave his chin and cheeks, brushing his hair. She'd helped Arietta with her dress; ever since their chat, his cousin had been really nice to her. How ironic his family members warmed up to her and treated her as if she'd joined the gang, when it was all useless if Marco didn't. Tonight would be their last in Italy, and in a matter of days, she'd no longer be needed to warm his bed.

Nico walked by her, carrying a flute of champagne and talking to a beautiful woman who strolled beside him. Lily lifted her hand to greet him, and he raised his flute with a kind smile. For the first time since he'd met him, he didn't seem like he saw right through her lies. *Either I'm getting better at it, or he's already drunk.*

A waitress offered her some bubbly, and she took it. Why not? She drank it in one gulp, a refreshing sensation rolling down her throat, loosening her limbs.

"Excuse me," said a man behind her.

She turned to find Marco's father. She hadn't seen much of him, thankfully, during her stay. After all she heard about him, she had to gather her strength to keep from slapping his face. Her blood still boiled in her veins. "Yes?"

"I met you on the first night. You're Marco's bride-to-be."

Wishful thinking. She lifted her chin. "That's right."

"I regret we haven't talked much."

"Do you also regret not talking to your son?" she said, and immediately second-guessed her spontaneity. But shit, it was too late. She cleared her throat, stretching to her full height so the tall man wouldn't intimidate her. "I can't help but notice the two of you have barely exchanged any words in the last few days."

Calogero's face didn't give away much. Unlike his sons, he wasn't very expressive. When he spoke, he kept his eyes hooded, his expression neutral. "Patricia, is it? You're quite forthcoming, given you just met me."

"I know enough about you."

"Ah. Marco's musings," he said, his wrinkles creasing around his eyes. "His world turned upside when his mother died, and our relationship never recovered from it. Doesn't mean I don't wish him well. I keep my distance because we don't have a lot in common anymore."

"A lot in common? He's your son," she said, remembering her sweet father and how they could look at each other and know what the other was thinking. They didn't always agree on everything, but when it came down to it, he had her back.

"Yes, he is, and you obviously feel passionately about him. I wondered about you, a woman who came out of nowhere and managed to catch him. I hope you know what you signed up for. Marco isn't so easy to get along with on a day-to-day basis."

"How would you know? You two haven't talked in forever, and when he was a child and needed you the most, you preferred to be a coward and blame him for your wife's death."

He glanced around them, as if to ensure no one watched them, and said in a steady tone, "Stop there, young lady. I've been generous in entertaining your out-of-line suggestions. It has to come to an end."

"You know what? Your wife had a condition, but you're the one who's sick. Now, if you'll excuse me," she said, seeing red at the corner of her eyes as she strode through the crowd. Thankfully, because of the live band, none of the guests should have heard them. Unless someone saw them talking and read their body language, she was okay.

She didn't give two shits about what Marco's father thought about her, but she didn't want to ruin Nonna's birthday party. Arietta waved at her, and she hung out with some of the cousins, listening to funny stories about their childhood. She pretended to engage, but every so often she scanned the living area, searching for Marco. What if she confessed that she'd told his father off? God. Maybe she shouldn't. He would hate her.

He'd hate her for licking his emotional wounds and making a big deal about it. *He might even send me away, or cut our deal short.* One of the clauses in the contract stated he had the right to terminate the affair at any time without any particular reason. She'd still get her end of the bargain, but he'd reserved that right.

"Everything okay?" Arietta asked, pulling her from her worst-case-scenario pondering.

"Yeah, why?"

"You seem preoccupied."

"I'm wondering what Marco is up to. I haven't seen him for a while." Damn him. It was the party that had brought them to Italy, and now he disappeared?

"Oh, he's right there," she said, pointing at the opposite side of terrace. "He's been talking to Nonna for the past twenty minutes."

Twenty minutes. Had he seen her talking with his father? *If he doesn't mention anything, I won't.* She had to deal with saying goodbye to his family, to Italy, a place she probably wouldn't visit again. People she wouldn't ever see again. The notion stiffened her entire body. God, she had a hard time letting go of things.

During the rest of the party, she went through the motions. Family members made toasts and honored Debora. Dinner was served, and then the butler produced a huge cake. People ate, drank, laughed. She managed to keep good spirits and smile often to mask her growing sadness.

Going to the States meant she no longer needed to pretend to be Marco's fiancée. Damn it, she'd enjoyed the farce so much that she ended up believing in it.

After she and Marco said their goodbyes, they retreated to their suite. She opened the door to the balcony, staring at the lake. Stars peppered the dark sky, as the half-moon graced the night with all of her beauty.

Marco embraced her from behind, his arms sneaking around her, and she melted into him. "Who do you want to be tonight?" he whispered against her neck, causing all kinds of delicious tingles.

"I want us to be Lily and Marco," she said. She loved their games, their role plays, their creativity, but in the middle of so many lies, she needed to be true to the reality—he, Marco Giordano, was the man who weakened her knees. Who owned her heart, even if he didn't know it.

She turned around, glancing at him. He outlined her lips with his index finger, then when she thought he'd kiss her, he didn't. He traced the contours of her face as if using his hand to imprint the memory of her features in his mind. Maybe this was as hard for him as for her.

She entertained the notion, the impossible hope growing and rooting inside her like well-kept lawn. Resolute, she clung to the idea, adamant on showing him with her body how right they were for each other. She leaned into his caress, offering her entire being to him.

He dipped his head and captured her lips with his. The kiss grew slowly, steadily, provoking her body endlessly. Her nipples tightened; her pulse ran out of control. He caught her in his arms, much like a newlywed groom would, but with more hunger. A groan escaped his mouth, the primitive sound making her clit throb. She linked her arms around his head, intensifying the kiss, upping sexual anticipation between them.

Even when they tried to keep their hormones in check, the crazy, red-hot desire showed them who was in charge. He didn't lay her on the bed like the end of a fairy tale. He held her against the column of one of the embellished arches of the room. He nibbled her upper lip, then released it with a popping sound. She squirmed, already so aroused.

He hiked up her dress, provoking goose bumps on her bare flesh. She held him tighter, not wanting to let go. He rested his forehead against hers, and they shared a sigh. "You're extraordinary, Lily," he said. "Don't you ever forget it."

"You, too," she said, and fumbled to remove his jacket, her fingers trembling to open the buttons. Impatient, she held both sides of his crisp white shirt and ripped it apart. Hell, this was their last night in Italy. She had to show him how she felt about him.

He let out a growl, kissing her again, their tongues clashing, lips melding. She plastered herself to him, loving the feel of his warm, salty skin against hers. He reached to the zipper of her dress and lowered it until it reached her waist, bunching the fabric. Getting rid of the silk between her chest and his, she moaned, like her body had found a safe haven. A thrill shot from her breasts to the rest of her. She rubbed her breasts on his hair-dusted pecs, stealing a groan from him.

"If you were a drink, I'd be an alcoholic," he whispered.

"Marco..." she murmured, but he silenced her with the most ravenous kiss she'd ever received. She squirmed into him, breathless, so eager for him. He put his hands under her ass, lifting her up, and without disengaging from her mouth, took both of them to the bed. She fell on top of him, overwhelmed.

She kept him down and lifted herself enough to straddle him and nibble his chin. He lifted his own mouth to kiss her, but she withdrew, pushing him back into the mattress. "Let me fuck you."

She slid her hand down his body, snaking it into his

pants. Without wasting time to unbuckle and remove them completely, she lowered them along with his boxers enough— to his knees—and clasped his glorious cock. Didn't matter how many times she'd seen it... She loved that massive rod. She loved him.

She squeezed it, earning a deep moan from him.

"You're torturing me."

"Now you know what it's like to be me."

"I've known for a while," he said, and put her hand over his heart. She spread her fingers over it, feeling his pulse race madly, and a rush of adrenaline went through her. She— her touch, her presence—had an effect on him. What if she affected him more than she imagined?

Yelping with excitement, she lowered herself to him, planting little pecks on his nose, cheeks, and forehead. She moved her hand, touching his cock again, positioning him close to her then impaling herself with his massive dick. Oh, how she loved having him throb against her pussy, occupying every inch of her sex, branding her even when he wasn't trying. Filling her. Completing her.

"I love you, Marco." The truth escaped her mouth as she began to ride him. Her hand flew to her lips, and she realized it was too late to take it back.

Chapter Seventeen

I love you.

Her words almost pulled him from his foggy, aroused state. She moved swiftly, thrusting herself onto his dick, swaying her hips in a sensual dance he couldn't deny.

Maybe she didn't mean it and had said she loved him in the heat of the moment. Even though he didn't completely convince himself, he used the possibility to enjoy the sex without thinking.

He thrust his cock upward, and she took him, using her inner muscles to clench him. An insane throb dominated his body, knotting his whole being into one pulse. He had to close his eyes and will himself to wait to come.

Eager for more, he lifted his hands and cupped her tits. She threw her head back for a moment, and he touched her breasts, encircling the nipples with his fingers. She gazed at him, her eyes challenging him to respond to her spontaneous declaration of love.

He searched for undercurrents of fear or uncertainty or frustration but only found clarity in the depths of her green irises. His heart drummed in his chest, and he didn't know how to react. Luckily, his own body responded for him. As if entranced, he shifted his position so he sat on the mattress, legs crossed around her, without disengaging from her. Lily was still on top of him but much closer, his arms wrapped around her, bringing her to him.

That's when he knew. Fuck. She loved him.

He should call it quits immediately, leave the bed, and get her on the first flight back to the United States. But as she moved, each time undulating her hips so he'd hit a deeper part of her, he wanted to stay with her more than anything.

Groaning, he thrust into her, provoking a series of moans from her sinful lips. He upped his game, plummeting hard then retreating enough to make her squirm.

"Yes," she hissed out, her long eyelashes sweeping over her lids. "Yes. I love you. Oh, Marco… How I love you," she said.

Air rushed from his lungs. He only rammed her with more strength, unsure if he wished her words were truth or lies. Sweat broke out on his forehead, and then she kissed him in such a passionate way, for an instant he didn't remember where they were.

He matched her intensity, shoving his fingers into her hair and massaging her scalp, hoping to give her the same kind of short circuit he experienced whenever she touched him. She tightened her wet walls around his rod, and this time, he felt the building pressure in his core, his balls heavy and throbbing.

"Yes," she said when he momentarily came up for air. She bucked into him, hinting she was close. Without letting go of her hair, he used his free hand to slide down and flick her clit, working it relentlessly.

She shuddered, the vein on her neck pulsating and warning him she was coming. Responding to his own urges, he plunged one last time, unable to wait. His body contracted, then released, and he spilled his load inside her welcoming pussy. Fireworks exploded through him, the glorious sensation making waves until it had ridden his entire being, and his breathing became labored.

He kissed her forehead and eased her onto the mattress, when a sharp knock on the door made him extract himself from her and jump from the bed.

"What is it?" she whispered.

"Let me find out," he said, pulling on his pants. Quickly, he fetched his shirt from the floor, putting it on before opening the door.

"I'm sorry to disturb you, but we need to talk," his father said on the other side of the threshold.

He swallowed razors in his throat. Seeing his father this late at night meant something had gone wrong. "Wait," he ordered, then closed the door quickly to tell Lily, "I'll be right back." She nodded at him, her face confused, but he took advantage of her post-bliss state and slipped out of the room, shutting the door behind him.

He buttoned his shirt, walking alongside his father in the hall. Then his father came to a halt and told him, "Your grandmother has passed."

Marco froze, pinned to the spot, even though his knees threatened to buckle under his weight. Sadness welled up inside him, constricting his throat. Until now, he'd dealt with Nonna's weak heart as a fact, a certainty, and used a measure of practicality to cope. He looked at his father's expression—neutral as always, but his eyes seemed almost kind for a moment. Kind? Marco mocked inwardly. Why didn't his brother or Arietta break the news to him?

Tears he wouldn't have normally allowed fogged his field of vision. Marco wiped them with the back of his hand in a rough manner, but others replaced the ones dampening his skin. He remembered his grandmother's love for him, the sweet way she called his name, her genuine, positive outlook on life.

"I'm sorry," his father said, and planted a hand on his shoulder. Marco almost jerked away, driven by instinct, but his father pressed his palm into his shirt.

"Why did you come to tell me? Why not Nico?" Marco asked.

His father drew in a breath and then nodded to himself, as if realizing Marco's question made complete sense. Maybe Nico was calling the doctors, or making arrangements, and, out of convenience, someone had asked Calogero to notify Marco. Simple as that.

Calogero loosened his hold on him until he slid his hand off Marco completely. He opened his mouth, then hesitated. Marco looked into his father's dark eyes and found an emotion he had never seen before. A lump of frustration lodged in his throat.

"Because I'm sorry," his father said, his voice wavering.

His father opened his arms and hugged him, and Marco swallowed hard. He didn't want to believe his father, wasn't willing to forgive him so quickly. Yet, as Calogero kept clumsily embracing him, Marco tapped his back then slowly embraced him in return. Sorry wasn't enough, but it would do for now.

• • •

"Don't you want to come in?" Lily asked Marco when he motioned for her to enter her own house.

The past three days had been rough. They were supposed to return to the States sooner, but because of Nonna's death, Marco decided to stay longer and attend her funeral service. Lily supported him and didn't ask anything of him—

particularly after she had declared her love for him.

Marco followed her inside. He'd entered her apartment once or twice before, on much happier occasions. Now he had the painful task of ending their affair and breaking the contract he'd insisted on.

She put her bag on the couch and then washed her hands at the kitchen sink. During the flight home, he fooled her by pretending to work on his laptop, while what he was really doing was thinking about a hard conversation he had to have. He'd also kept his thoughts to himself during the drive to her place. The idea of having the driver take her in a separate car crossed his mind, but that would have broken her heart.

Not like what I'm about to do is any different.

When his brother had accused him of falling for her, he'd dismissed the idea. He couldn't have. That would have been careless. When she'd told him she loved him three days prior, he'd known for sure that she truly loved him. Being with her because she cared about his sexual desires was selfish, but that he could handle. Being with her because she loved him meant opening the door to a world of disappointment.

He hadn't been able to love his mother, or his father, even after he tried to mend fences following Nonna's death. Well, mend fences the Calogero way, by pretending he hadn't ruined his childhood, but that was beside the point. Hell, even his grandmother, whom he did love—he did a bad job of being there for her. He'd kept away for far longer than he should have. He had to save Lily from himself.

"Do you want anything to drink?" she asked.

He took a deep breath. "Lily, our agreement is coming to an end."

She tilted her head to the side, as if trying to understand if that was a good or bad thing. "What does this mean?"

"I no longer require you to continue to live up to your part of the bargain. You're released of all your duties, and I'll keep up my end of our deal."

Tears rolled down from her eyes before she parted her lips. A side of him simmered with anger, anger at himself. His gut grew tight, but he had to keep his resolve. If he wavered, all would be lost. *She* would be lost.

"Just like that? You're releasing me of my duties?" she said, pain lacing her words.

His throat pulsed, and he had to convince himself to move on with his plan, for her sake and happiness, even if it seemed like he was doing the opposite. "This has been the agreement from the beginning. I never wanted to hurt you, Lily. That's why I had a contract."

"You didn't want to hurt yourself. That's why you needed a piece of paper to keep from getting close."

A knot formed in his gut, and each time he glanced at her, the knot twisted painfully. "I'm sorry. I can't give you anything else. I never promised I would."

"Another easy way out for you. You can shove your so-called honesty up your ass. I doubt you're being honest right now. You're going to stand here in my home and tell me you're totally fine with letting me go? That you don't feel anything for me other than sexual chemistry?"

He paced, shoving his trembling fingers into his pockets to keep them from view. "What I feel doesn't matter. Feelings don't have an IQ. I need to follow my instinct."

She grabbed a box of tissues from her countertop and used them to wipe the tears from her glossy, achingly sad eyes. He had to wrestle the need to erase the distance between them and hug her tightly.

"Your instincts suck. And you know what?" She crumpled the tissue and tossed it to the floor, then locked her eyes with his. "You're not honest. You're afraid."

He exhaled. "I'm rational. Trust me, I'm making a decision for the both of us that you'll thank me for later."

"Is this because I told you I loved you?"

"No," he lied. He'd hate for her to rehash what she'd said later on her own. She hadn't done or said anything wrong, anyway. "It's over."

"When I met you, I thought you were this powerful man who fought for what he wanted. Then I learned you fought against your own emotions because they'd hurt you through the years. Now I see a coward who's not even willing to fight for what he deserves. You're too set in your own little world of games and documents."

"That's right," he said.

"Get out of my home," she said, stretching to her full height. Despite the tears, and the melancholy in her voice, there was a challenge in her eyes he didn't dare to accept. "I was always okay with you being broken, but I'm not good with you being a coward."

. . .

"Honey, I love all my gifts. You shouldn't have," her mother said, glancing at all the souvenir knickknacks and shirts Lily had bought in Italy. "But I'm so glad you did," her mother said with a wink, then played with a small key ring.

Lily willed herself to smile. After Marco had left her apartment, she'd given herself three full days before visiting her mother. To conceal her puffy red eyes, she'd put on a godawful amount of makeup.

"What's wrong?" her mother asked, sitting next to her on the opposite bed. Lily was glad her mother's roommate had left for an aqua aerobics class and they could be alone.

Crap. Her mother knew her too well, so saying nothing was out of question.

"A couple of different things. I did meet a handsome Italian man, who ended up not returning my feelings." Or he was too afraid to admit them. Sadness welled in her throat, but she swallowed the dry lump, determined to continue the clean version of what had happened, even if her voice trembled, a thread away from breaking completely. "He lives in New York, but…it's complicated."

His mother withdrew. "Is he married?"

"No. No."

"Then the war isn't lost, my dear. Either he needs time to get to know you better, or he's a fool."

For the past couple of days, Lily had called him every name in the book—fool hadn't been one of them. He'd been a fucking coward. Maybe he didn't love her the same way as she did him, but crap, she knew he had strong feelings for her. She'd felt it in his possession, had seen it in his eyes. "He's a big fool who doesn't want complications."

"Those are the biggest fools. You said two things—that you had something else to tell me. What is it?"

"Well, I was able to save the salon. I didn't want to tell you before, but it wasn't doing well. Financially."

Her mother took her hand in hers and gave it a gentle tug. "Honey, I'm so sorry," she said. "Why didn't you tell me sooner?"

"Because you were so excited every time you mentioned it. That salon is the last thing left of the family I once had, of my childhood. I didn't want it to slip away."

"Honey, that's not true. I love the salon with every fiber of my being, but I hope your father and I left you with more than that," she said, lifting her hand and briefly touching Lily's heart. "Remember our first family trip to Coney Island? How every winter we drove up north to pick up a Christmas tree? How sad we became when you decided you no longer needed good-night stories? You must have been ten or eleven."

"Eleven."

"There you go. All these memories you can take with you

anywhere you go."

"You're making me cry." Just when she'd vowed not to lose it in front of her mother.

"It's okay. Come here." Her mother wrapped her in a hug. "Now, tell me, are those two things related—the man who broke your heart and the business? Did he try to take your business from you, or save it?"

Crap. Mom had read enough Agatha Christie mystery novels back in the day to see right through bullshit. She cleared her throat. She should have felt triumphant at saving the business, keeping everything afloat. But having Marco leave her had the opposite effect. Her mother propped her to sit straight, and looked into her eyes.

"You're going to tell me everything."

• • •

"I'm here to see Mr. Giordano," Lily said to the receptionist. "Mr. Nicola Giordano," she said, this time to herself.

"Of course. Just a moment," the woman said as she pressed a finger on the tiny earpiece.

Lily had called Nicola's assistant about an hour before, requesting a meeting with him. She'd expected to wait a lot longer, but Marco's brother had agreed on seeing her immediately.

Telling her mother the truth a day earlier hadn't been easy. But now she knew why saving the salon weighed so heavily on her shoulders. She'd used her body to save her business. She'd ended up compromising her heart, as well, but it didn't feel right. Marco no longer contacted her, and despite how he'd acted, she knew their time together had been more than a business transaction for him. He just wasn't willing to accept it.

As the receptionist gave her a badge and gave her

instructions, Lily simply nodded. She hadn't eaten much lately, and unlike the first time she went to his office, today she had no intention of seducing Marco. Fresh faced and with her hair in a ponytail, she exited the elevator on the top floor and nodded when Nico's assistant instructed her to enter his office.

Apprehension settled in her stomach. What if she ran into Marco? God, that'd be beyond awkward.

"Nico. Hi," she said as she strode into his office.

He stood from his chair. "Nice to see you, Lily. Please have a seat," he said, gesturing at the leather chair in front of him.

She walked through his enormous space until she found the chair and then sat. Only then did he sit. He grabbed a pen from a holder and clicked it. "I have to say, I'm curious about your visit. What brings you here?"

She crossed her legs then uncrossed them. In her head, she had played how this would roll a few times on her drive over there. Now her stomach churned with nervousness. "You know the beauty shop I own? The one you and your brother needed so badly to build a garage?"

Nico's green eyes studied her. "Yes, of course."

She stared at him in silence. Those Giordano guys certainly didn't make it easy for the New York women. Nico was just as dashingly handsome as Marco, though he didn't provoke in her the same reactions his brother did. She took a deep, long breath and said, "When your brother first talked to me, he really needed my space. I didn't want to sell, but I've changed my mind."

"You have?" He leaned closer, his brows furrowing. "Are you upping your price?"

"No. I'd like to sell it and donate the proceeds to a cancer foundation in my father's name," she said, her shoulders dropping a notch. Her arms relaxed, and she felt good about her decision to let go of the past and focus on the future. She'd accused Marco of being a coward, but was she any different, clinging to her old way of life instead of making room for the new?

Nico scratched the back of his neck, his expression a tad skeptical. As a businessman, she imagined he wouldn't understand why she'd sell after everything she'd gained, and without asking for higher value. "Why the sudden change of heart?"

"Because I have a hard time letting go of things, and this is my first lesson."

"Why contact me?"

"Because you need the location. I admit, it's not like you'll use it for anything exciting, but that's not my problem."

"Have you told my brother about it?"

"No." She didn't want to face Marco again, not after the abrupt way they ended things. She surged to her feet and continued, "You don't have to tell him about my visit. You can tell him whatever you want. Have your people contact me with a price. I'll give them the information for where they can donate the money. We can deal with signing the contract, etcetera, then you transfer the funds to the charity. I am going to need evidence the transfer was made."

He stood as well. "No problem."

"Thanks. That's all," she said, nodding. She'd have to move forward to a life without the salon, and without Marco. Somehow, saying goodbye to the shop seemed a lot easier than knowing she'd never get to kiss Marco Giordano again.

Chapter Eighteen

"Damn it. Where's the Patterson file?" Marco asked himself, his fingers flying over the keyboard. He pressed the intercom button. "Claire, get me some coffee, please."

"Again?" she asked.

He shook his head. So it was his fourth cup that morning. Who cared? "Yes."

In the past few days, he'd dived into work to forget about walking out on Lily. His fingers itched to call her every time he saw his cell phone. *He* itched to man up and go see her, take back all the nonsense he'd fed her—and himself. What if, deep down, she agreed with him? She didn't need a man as cowardly as he'd been by her side.

He'd been such a wimp he hadn't yet opened the letter his grandmother wrote for him. After her death, the butler found letters she'd left inside her nightstand for her grandkids and other family members. She apparently wrote them a couple of days prior to the party because she'd known she didn't have much time left. Marco carried his with him, inside his suit, and its presence gave him a sense of comfort he didn't want to part with.

"Your assistant asked me bring you this," Nico said, pointing at the coffee mug he carried as he strolled into his office.

"Thanks," he said, rubbing his eyes.

Nico placed the mug on his desk, and Marco fetched it right away, lifting it to his lips. "When was the last time you slept? Or shaved?"

Marco chugged down the coffee then set down the cup. "I've been busy."

"Yes. Your assistant said you've practically lived here for the last few days."

Marco stretched his arms. "Why do you care?"

Nico didn't sit. He loitered, leaning against the desk, arms folding as he gave his brother a glance that told him he wouldn't drop the subject easily.

"What?"

"Lily came to see me yesterday."

At the mention of her name, his heart skipped a beat, only to resume a second later, faster than ever. "You?"

"Yeah." Nico opened the folder he carried and laid it on the desk. "She wants to sell her salon to us."

Sell? This didn't seem like Lily at all. Marco shortened the gap between them, launching himself at his brother, pulling his collar. "If you bullied her into selling it to you, God help me, I'll beat the shit out of you," he said, knowing not only were they the same height, but had similar set of martial art skills.

Nico didn't move an inch. He stared at him with a glint of amusement in his eyes. Marco's fingers loosened on his collar until his arms dropped to his sides. "Wow. You really got it bad, baby brother."

Damn Nico. He knew how much Marco hated the *baby brother* crap. "Fuck off. Before you do, tell me exactly what happened," he said. The Lily he knew—the Lily he loved—would never give up the salon that meant so much to her. She loved the place. Why on Earth would she do it?

"Tell me," he hissed.

His brother lifted his hands in surrender. "Fine. I meant what I said. I didn't go looking for her. I had even already talked to some disgruntled investors. Anyway, she showed up in my office and offered her salon. I was surprised at first, but I sent her a contract to make sure she wasn't playing me, using the shop as a lure to get more money."

"She wasn't."

"Nope. She wants all the money to be donated to her charity of choice. And she asked me not to tell you anything. Of course, in life we can't have everything, so here I am."

Marco shook his head. "You aren't going through with this. I forbid you."

Nico shrugged. "Why? I didn't twist her arm; she came to me. There is no one in our way."

"She can't… That place means everything for her. I need to talk to her."

"Well, I'm supposed to go inspect it tonight, after a meeting. Maybe I'll let her know what you think," Nico said, then smoothed his tie. He strolled to the door, and Marco could tell his brother waited for him to say something. To stop him. He saw Nico leave and close the door behind him, like he had dropped by only to feed him the news.

He reached for the letter buried in the inside pocket of his suit and touched the envelope. The corners of the heavy paper curled, a sign he had played with it long enough, ever since he'd received it. Why did Lily want to sell the salon, and worse, not keep the profits? None of it made sense.

With the tips of his fingers unsteady, he opened the envelope, retrieving the stationary paper with his nonna's strong, cursive handwriting. He touched the paper before reading, trying to understand why he associated it with Lily.

His pulse raced as he began to read the short note written in Italian.

"My dear Marco,

Tomorrow I will give your Patricia the necklace that belonged to your mother. I don't know if I'll be around to see her wearing it, but I want her to have it. I know life didn't hand you a good start, and many times I blamed myself for your unhappiness. There were many days I wished I had taken you out of your father's home and raised you myself.

I did try once to talk to him into it, but he refused. I should have tried harder. I should have contacted the authorities—those thoughts have always haunted me.

I thought I'd never see you embracing love. When I met Patricia, I saw how you looked at her, and to know you've taken the plunge, that you have decided to pursue your own joy, makes me happier than you can ever imagine.

If this letter reaches you, that means I've left and have encountered your mother. I'll tell her about the smart, successful, caring man you've become. I'll tell her, despite the cards you were dealt, you aren't afraid anymore.

Love you more than anything,

Nonna."

Marco sank into the chair, dropping the letter to the floor. His limbs felt weak and loose in contrast to the heavy weight expanding in his chest. His heart throbbed in his temple, pounding his veins more than any migraine ever had.

I'll tell her, despite the cards you were dealt, you aren't afraid anymore. He could almost hear his grandmother's voice saying those words. He thrust his hands into his hair, hoping to ease down the agony consuming him.

Lily is right. I've been a coward. "A coward," he said out loud, as if it would bring any sort of clarity about his actions. She could have used giving up her business as an excuse to see him, or hell, even blackmail him—emotionally or monetarily.

That wasn't his Lily. She was kind, generous, honest. Maybe he'd known that all along but preferred not to believe it, because knowing a woman like her genuinely loved him made it hard for him not to love her back.

He swallowed the lump in his throat. He loved her…and he'd been a fool not to learn the one lesson she'd taught him even without enunciating the words—courage. She'd fought for her salon. She'd fought for truth the entire time they were together, getting him to speak about the past he'd thought he'd buried. Hell, she'd even fought for him when she told him she'd fallen for him.

A rush of adrenaline bolted through him, urging him to surge to his feet. Determination filled his heart.

It's high time I started fighting for her.

• • •

Lily clutched her bag. Shit, she was running late. She'd spent the day sending out resumes and scheduling interviews at bigger, coveted salons where she'd love to work. Then, Nico texted her and asked her to come to his office. Then, another message from Nico told her about a change of plans. She must go to her salon ASAP because he had some issues he needed to discuss, important setbacks that could halt the negotiations.

Whatever. Who cared, if they were going to demolish the place anyway? By the time she arrived, most of the businesses around her were either quieter than usual or already closed. Some of them had asked for a grace period after selling to Nico, while others were already operating elsewhere.

She reached for her bag to retrieve her keys and open the glass door, then she noticed the door was opened a notch. What? Did Nico let himself in, and maybe wanted to prove a point about low security? Still didn't make sense, though. Even if he had found big foundation problems with the area, it wouldn't matter if they planned do away with the strip mall completely.

Sighing, she walked in. Dozens of small, lit candles were scattered everywhere...on the shelves, on her counter, on the floor. The scent of lilies inundated the place, and she noticed several vases of flowers embellishing the space, blending with the fragrance of the candles. What the hell? Did Nico think he could just seduce her since his brother was out of the picture?

"Nico?"

The door to the supply room opened. "Marco?" she called.

Marco walked up to her in silence, so focused. His hair had been freshly washed and his face shaven, but she didn't miss the dark circles under his eyes. Had he been as miserable as she? "Why did you decide to sell the shop?" he asked.

She switched her weight from foot to foot. Why did he care? Yet, he had come to see her, so maybe her selling it impacted him in a greater way. Or, he was just thanking her with the flowers? He could have had someone send those to her. Money didn't mean much to him. She tried to tell herself not to expect much from him. That didn't ease the throbbing at the base of her throat.

"It didn't seem right to keep it. Before our trip, our deal, I wanted to save the salon at all costs. Then, after you left me that way, it dawned on me that if I had to do so much to keep the salon, then maybe I should use it as a lesson in letting go."

"You don't have to let go. I told my brother I'll raise hell if he buys it from you."

She clamped her lips. She could take advantage of his generosity, but the idea of creating brand new memories seduced her. Saying goodbye to the place that had made her childhood and young life so happy wouldn't be easy, but she needed to face reality. She wasn't a savvy businesswoman. She was a talented hairdresser who would love to have more time to learn her craft without worrying about financial overheads. "That's my decision. Not yours."

"True. I just needed to make sure the decision has been yours all along, and no one convinced you to sell it."

She clapped her hands together. "Well, now you know it. Your conscience is clear. What are you doing here anyway?"

"I'm here for you, Lily."

She shook her head, confused. Did he mean he wanted them to be friends? She wasn't ready to be buddies with him—she never would be. "You made it clear there's no place in your life for me, that I'd be better off without you."

"You see, maybe I was right. You can be better off without me, but I'm no good without you. I've fallen for you, and it took me long enough to understand that feeling made me stronger, not weaker."

Did he just say he loves me? Her head spun, and she clutched the back of the chair for support. "What makes you think I'll believe you? Or you won't change your mind tomorrow?" she asked, proud of herself for giving him a hard time when instinct willed her in his arms.

"I won't change my mind." He took a velvety box from his pocket and opened it to her. "I'm offering you a different contract, with a lifetime of commitment."

She glanced at the diamond ring sparkling in the box. She'd returned the engagement ring he bought her in Italy and the necklace his grandmother gave her via courier, but this was a different one. "Why another one?"

"Because there is nothing false about what I'm proposing. From the beginning, everything needs to be new and honest."

She worried her bottom lip. A strand of excitement moved through her. Was this really happening after all? He loved her…and wanted to be with her forever. "Will it include hot sex?"

"Daily. Some days, hourly. It'll also include partnership, friendship, and lots of sharing."

"When you put it like that."

"I don't deserve your love, but I'll do everything in my power to earn it. I'll fight for it with everything I've got."

"How about starting right now?"

He kissed her, and for minutes their mouths worked together, their tongues stroking each other with reckless abandon. Oh, how she'd missed him… She plastered her body to his, and she caught a whiff of his manly scent—a scent she'd inhale, now, every day of her life.

He pulled her into the supply room and closed the door behind him. She chuckled. A few of the products she hadn't boxed fell to the floor, but she didn't care. She linked her arms around his neck, and he lifted her legs so she wrapped them around his torso.

"I told you once I wasn't sure I'd ever get over you," he said, placing her above the sink. She fumbled to open the buttons of his shirt, settling for yanking it open, the buttons flying in the air. "I want to get inside you, on top of you, under you, but never, ever, over you."

She snatched him closer and lifted her head to lock their lips. The familiar need that came whenever she was around him poked at her, her insides burning for him. A moan made its way up her throat, but he swallowed it, their craving for each other only letting them catch their breath every so often.

Marco disengaged the kiss to stare deep in her eyes. Heat coiled at the pit of her stomach, but also a much more permanent feeling—happiness. "I love you, Lily Jenkins."

"I love you, too, Marco," she said, knowing he was the one thing she'd never let go.

About the Author

Carmen Falcone learned at an early age that fantasizing about fictional characters beat doing math homework any day. Brazilian by birth and traveler by nature, she moved to Central Texas after college and met her broody Swiss husband, living proof that opposites attract. She found in writing her deepest passion and the best excuse to avoid the healthy lifestyle everyone keeps talking about. When she is not lost in the world of romance, she enjoys spending time with her two kids, being walked by her three crazy pugs, reading, catching up with friends, and chatting with random people in the checkout line.

If you love erotica, one-click these hot Scorched releases...

IMPROPER PROPOSAL
a Dossier novella by Cathryn Fox

Billionaire Will Thomas is back in England for a big surprise. Could Harper be it? One thing he is sure of...he wants her for himself. It's been a long time since he's been attracted to a woman like this. Harper takes one look at Will and her body burns. He's tall, hot, and looks at her with hunger in his eyes. But giving in to their desires means all kinds of complications for them both...

BURNED
a Viking Bastards novel by Christina Phillips

I offered her everything, and she threw it back in my face. Now she's back, for one week only, gorgeous, successful, and I can't keep away. She offers a way to heal our fractured past. She burned me so bad––there's no way I should even want to be near her. But the more she gives, the more I need. Until I discover the real reason she left, and my whole damn world implodes...

HIS FOR THE WEEK
a novel by Alice Gaines

Sex columnist Désirée "Rae" Knight is in a bind—and not the kind she usually likes. Her newest assignment, and possible big break, is an article for her magazine on the sex resort that just opened. The only problem is it's couples only. Although she writes about having red-hot sex, she's been single longer than she'd like to admit. Enter her coffee shop crush, who she's been secretly ogling every morning. Trouble is, he doesn't know she exists.

73727131R00111